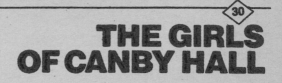

THE GIRLS
OF CANBY HALL

30

SURPRISE!

EMILY CHASE

P9-BBT-498

SCHOLASTIC INC.
New York Toronto London Auckland Sydney

ISBN 0-590-41672-3

Copyright © 1988 by Lynn Zednick All rights reserved. Published by Scholastic Inc. THE GIRLS OF CANBY HALL is a registered trademark of Scholastic Inc.

12 11 10 9 8 7 6 5 4 3 2 1   8 9/8 0 1 2 3/9

Printed in the U.S.A.   01

First Scholastic Printing, October 1988

THE GIRLS
OF CANBY HALL

30

SURPRISE!

THE GIRLS OF CANBY HALL

CHAPTER ONE

Andrea Cord kicked at the fallen leaves as she cut across the lawn of Canby Hall. The afternoon sun caught her shiny black hair and set it shimmering. Andrea scanned the campus and sighed deeply. It was already October. Fall had come to Canby Hall.

Andy sat on a bench beneath one of the big old trees and looked overhead at the leaves that were beginning to turn to red and gold. Those that had fallen early were already brown and dry beneath her feet.

Andy could feel herself right on the edge of depression. She'd had those feelings off and on ever since she'd hurt her foot a few weeks ago — even though she knew she'd be able to dance again.

She took a deep breath and stood up. She would not let herself sit here and become morose. Andy looked toward the student center. Maybe something fun was going on over there.

But the student center was nearly deserted. Two girls were sitting at a far table, but the afternoon sun reflecting off the glass was temporarily blinding and Andy wasn't able to recognize them.

Going over to the bulletin board, she began to read the notices. Someone wanted a ride to Boston. Someone else wanted a tutor in calculus. Andy moved on past those. She had neither a car to take to Boston nor the mind to tutor calculus. Then her eyes caught another notice.

"Wanted: Interested students to work on the committee for the upcoming Halloween party. See Meredith Pembroke for details."

What a great idea! She was sure her two roommates, Toby and Jane, would want to do that. They needed something to pick them up a little, too, Andy suspected. And since Meredith Pembroke was the housemother for Baker where the three of them shared Room 407, Andy was sure Meredith would welcome their help. Andy decided to go see Meredith right away.

When Andy turned around, she came face to face with Gigi Norton, who'd slipped up behind Andy and was reading the notice over Andy's shoulder. Gigi was taller, with the athletic build of someone usually involved in Canby Hall athletics. But Gigi wasn't the kind of girl to get involved in anything unless it was something mean and rotten. Last year, she had given a "come as someone you hate" party that no one attended except her faithful sidekick, Yolanda. She and Yolanda must have been the girls sitting at the table near the windows when Andy came in.

"Well, Andrea, have you been doing any dancing lately?" Gigi asked, exchanging a knowing look with Yolanda.

"Yes, I have," Andy said with a forced smile. "My foot is so much better that I have an audition with the New York City Ballet during Christmas." She pushed her way between the two girls. "You'll have to excuse me. I have so much to do to get ready."

Gigi watched Andy leave the student center. Yolanda turned to her only friend. "Gosh, she must be really good."

"You dork! She was lying. I've seen her dance. She couldn't make the New York City Ballet if she had therapy for both ankles and bionic legs attached." Yolanda giggled. Sometimes Gigi did mean things that were hard for her to go along with, but there were other times when she was *so* funny.

"Let's see what captured the interest of Miss Goody-Two Shoes up here." Gigi began to read the notices. She skipped over the first two just like Andrea had done. Then her eyes settled on the notice for the Halloween party. Gigi looked at the bulletin board again. Her face lit up. "Come on," she said grabbing Yolanda by the arm. You and I are about to volunteer for the Halloween party committee."

"Ooo, fun."

"It certainly will be," Gigi said. She smiled to herself as she thought of all the havoc she could wreak on those Baker House babies who thought they ran the school.

"Guess what, you guys?" Andy said bursting through the door of 407 Baker House. "We're going to be on the committee for the Halloween Dance!"

"We? Who's we?" Jane asked, looking up from her desk. Her long blonde hair framed her classically pretty features.

"We. Me, you, and Toby."

"Whoa, there, I'm not so sure I want to get involved with any kind of committee where you have to go to meetings and sit around making dumb decisions. There's not a lot of time left for me to enjoy the outdoors. It's almost winter," Toby said, thinking about last year when the snow felt so overwhelming that they'd finally planned a Winter Blahs party to break the monotony of it. "I'd much rather be riding Max while the weather's good enough to do it."

Toby was from Rio Verde, Texas, and while she hadn't been able to bring Texas with her, she'd found the next best thing when she stumbled onto the Crowell place. Randy Crowell and Toby had formed a strong friendship based on a mutual love of horses, and Toby spent a good deal of time out at the ranch.

"With the school newspaper, I don't know if I have time for any more commitments," Jane sighed.

"Boy, that's just great," Andy said, flopping down on the bed. "Since when are you guys are too busy for a party?"

"Just because we're busy doesn't mean that you can't be involved," Jane said.

"And what fun will that be? It's been so long since we've done anything fun together, I almost feel like we're just roommates these days. What happened to friendship?"

"Well, I guess it wouldn't kill me to miss an afternoon or two at Randy's," Toby said slowly.

"And I suppose I could take some time away from the paper," Jane conceded.

"That's terrific!" Andy jumped off the bed. "I knew I could count on you. It'll be so much fun. Come on. Let's go tell Meredith we want to be on the committee."

Andy had already disappeared from the

room before Toby and Jane had gotten to their feet. "I really don't have time for this," Jane said under her breath to Toby.

"Yeah, but did you see that look on Andy's face? This is the most excited she's been in weeks. And, who knows, maybe it'll be fun."

Andy was already knocking at Meredith's door when Jane and Toby came up behind her. The door opened and Meredith stood in the doorway in a red sweat suit, her brown hair tied back with a red and white scarf. What a contrast it was to the stuffy woman who had come here last year in the business suits and proper buns that made her appear to be a younger clone of the headmistress, Patrice Allardyce!

"We saw the notice on the bulletin board in the student center, and we want to work on the Halloween party," Andy said.

"Come in, girls. What a busy place I have this afternoon."

The three girls stepped into the room, only to be greeted by Gigi and Yolanda who were sitting comfortably on Meredith's couch.

"What are you guys doing here?" Andy asked.

"The same thing you are, I imagine," Gigi said. "Volunteering our services for the Halloween party. After all, I have given several parties, and I know quite a bit about planning them."

"Right," Jane said. "Now if you could just get people to come to them after you were finished planning them. . . ."

"Excuse me," Meredith said, "could we get on with it?"

"Yes, we certainly could," Jane said shooting an icy stare at her former roommate. Jane had had the bad misfortune to have Gigi assigned to her as a roommate her first year at Canby Hall, and Jane had come to think of her less than fondly as The Worst Person in the World.

"We only have a week and a half. Can the five of you meet tomorrow about four o'clock?"

"We can," Andy said.

"And so can we," Gigi said. The two of them looked like two captains squaring off before a game. Gigi got up from the couch. "Well, we'd better go. I'm really looking forward to working with you, Ms. Pembroke."

"Call me Meredith."

"Of course. Anyway, I can't tell you how excited I am. I have so many great ideas that it'll breathe new life into some of the dull parties we've had around here in the past." She looked at Jane, Toby, and Andy. "No offense, girls, I guess you were on some of the planning committees, weren't you?"

"Well, then, tomorrow it is," Meredith said, opening the door for the girls. Andy,

Toby, and Jane followed Yolanda and Gigi out into the hall.

"This ought to be lots of fun," Gigi said. "I just love Halloween. I'm sure I can plan the perfect party, in spite of the handicap of working with people who have less experience than I do in these matters."

"That's right. Planning the perfect Halloween party should be pretty easy for a witch," Jane said. Toby inhaled sharply. She still remembered all the trouble Gigi had caused last year when they had been planning the Winter Blahs party. Gigi had sunk so low as to steal Andy's term paper and write Toby's friend Neal a nasty letter signed by Andy. There wasn't much she wouldn't try to get even.

"Eat your heart out, Janie. With my help, this just may be the best party Canby Hall has ever seen." Gigi went on down the stairs, followed by Yolanda, who, as usual, had let Gigi do all the talking for both of them.

"Well, that settles it," Jane said. "Even if we don't have the time to be on the Halloween committee, we'll have to make time. There's no way I would back down and let Gigi and Yolanda plan this party."

They were walking past Dee and Maggie's room when their voices drifted in. "What party?" Dee called out to them.

"Hi, guys," Andy said, pushing the door open. "We went up to volunteer for the

Halloween party committee and guess who else was there?"

"Who?" Maggie said, pushing up her glasses, which were always sliding down her petite nose.

"Gigi and Yolanda!"

"I can just imagine the kind of party they'd plan," Maggie said with a shudder. "Dee, I think we need to do a little volunteering ourselves." Maggie got up from the bed where she had been sitting cross-legged with her books spread all around her.

"Yeah, that would be great," Andy said. "With five to two at least that'll even the odds in our favor."

"There is no such thing as even odds when you're dealing with Gigi," Jane said.

"And I actually thought this was going to be fun," said Toby, who had been more than unusually quiet. She had an all too vivid memory of Gigi's cruelty. In fact, Gigi was one of the few people who could intimidate Toby. With Toby's tall stature and her fiery red hair, she was the one who did most of the intimidating. But unlike Gigi Norton, Toby's intimidation of others was totally accidental.

CHAPTER TWO

Meredith Pembroke looked indiscreetly at her watch. Was it only four twenty-one? The way these girls had been going at each other it felt like she had been locked in this room with them for the past week. More precisely, she had felt like a referee in a boxing match between two very aggressive rivals.

Listening to the girls go at each other, she was glad Gigi didn't live in her dorm. She was one thoroughly unpleasant girl.

"Well, if we're going to hire a band, I think we should get somebody decent for a change," Gigi said as she flipped her long black hair. "Every time anyone has a party we end up with that stupid punk band, Ambulance."

Gigi looked directly at Jane. She knew full well that Jane's boyfriend, Cary, was the lead singer of Ambulance. Jane gritted her teeth. "Great, Gigi, do you know of a better band?"

"Not right off hand. But finding someone better than Ambulance shouldn't be that difficult. And I think having a D.J. play records would be a lot of fun, too. That way we could dance to all the latest songs and not have to listen to some amateur band slaughtering somebody else's hit beyond recognition."

"Before this goes any further," Meredith said, "Maybe we'd better consider the matter of money. Jane, you talk to Ambulance and find out how much they would charge, and Gigi, you call around and see how much it would cost to get a D.J."

The girls nodded in frosty agreement to Meredith's plan. Meredith picked up the plate of cookies. "Now, would anyone care for a cookie?" Only Toby reached out and took a handful of the peace offering.

Meredith looked around, almost hating to bring up the next point. It had taken them nearly a half an hour just to argue about whether or not to use a band. Meredith thought about the list of things they still had to discuss. At this rate, they might finish up the plans for the Halloween party by the Christmas holidays.

"Now, what kind of theme do you want

to use?" Meredith asked. Then she settled back and prepared for the fight. She didn't have to wait long.

"You know, I think a fairy tale theme would be fun," Dee suggested. Gigi snorted her disapproval. "No, wait. Everyone could dress like a favorite fairy tale character, and we could try and guess who they were. You know, a costume party."

"Yeah, a costume party for the *Sesame Street* gang," Gigi commented. Yolanda giggled.

"Got a better suggestion?" Jane asked.

"How about a *Friday the Thirteenth* theme? Come as your favorite character from a horror movie," Gigi said.

"That's no fair," Jane said. "Some of you will have a much better chance at being horrible than the rest of us."

"Girls. Girls!" Meredith said, before the fighting could go any further. "Why not just leave it up to the individual as to what kind of costume he or she would like to wear?"

"But that's so ordinary," Andy said. "That's the kind of thing you do every Halloween. I liked the idea of having a theme."

"Okay, then," Toby said, speaking up for the first time that afternoon, "why not dress up as your favorite movie or TV character, and then everyone will be happy."

"That's a great idea," Meredith said quickly. "It's settled then," she said, without giving anyone a chance for discussion.

"I still say it won't be a Halloween party unless there's something scary about it," Gigi pouted.

"Well, you're going, aren't you?" Andy asked.

"Look, what is the problem here? I've never seen you like this before."

"Sorry," Andy mumbled.

"Now, we'll need someone to be in charge of getting a group together to do the decorations," Meredith said.

"Let Jane," Maggie said. "She's great at that kind of stuff."

"Okay, Jane, you handle the decorations."

"Why doesn't Jane do the table decorations, and we'll handle the haunted house," Gigi volunteered.

"Who said anything about a haunted house?" Dee wanted to know.

"Well, you can't very well have a Halloween party without a haunted house," Gigi said.

"I guess you're right."

"Well, what do you know, one of the Baker House bunch finally agrees with me on something," Gigi said sarcastically.

"Look, girls, I know it would be a lot of fun to just go on arguing for another hour or so, but I have things to do, and I'm sure you all do, too, so why don't we end this meeting? Besides, I think we've covered quite a bit for today."

The girls began gathering their glasses and plates and carrying them to the kitchen. Meredith noticed that Gigi sat on the couch and let Yolanda take her dishes to the kitchen. It was really irritating to Meredith.

Andy flopped on her bed with Dee sitting down beside her. "I don't even know why Gigi volunteered for this committee in the first place."

"I do," Jane said. "To make our lives miserable."

"Then let's not let her do it to us," Toby said. "Face it, to someone like Gigi, her biggest joy in life is bringing misery to others. She's a perpetual rain cloud who goes around ruining everyone else's sunshine. We can't let her do it."

"What do you suggest we do?" Andy asked. "Hire an assassin or just back off and let her plan the whole thing?"

"I can just imagine the kind of party she'd plan," Jane said from the chair at her desk.

"No, she wants to do a haunted house. Let her do it. We'll make everything else so great that it won't matter what she does to louse things up. And, more importantly, it'll keep her out of our hair while we're planning the rest of the party."

"What a great idea," Andy said. She leaned back against the wall and relaxed for the first time since she'd walked into Meredith's apartment and come face to face with Gigi the Terrible.

Gigi was almost sprinting across the Canby Hall campus, talking furiously to Yolanda, who was struggling to keep up with her. "They think they'll run this whole thing just like every other party around here, but they've got another think coming."

"Gigi, could we slow down a little," Yolanda puffed as she jogged along beside her.

"Just keep up with me or get lost. I don't need to drag you or anybody else around. If I have to do this alone, I'll do it." Yolanda had the feeling Gigi was referring to a lot more than their afternoon sprint back to Addison, where they lived.

"They want to turn this into another Boston Tea Party just like every other boring thing that stuffy Jane Barrett of Boston comes in contact with. Well, not this time."

Gigi slowed down and grabbed Yolanda's arm in a vise-like hold. "Let them do the rest of the Mickey Mouse decorations. We're going to do that haunted house. And it will really be something to remember. When we're finished, people will be talking about it for years to come — *long* after everyone has forgotten who those snobs in 407 were, let alone what kind of stupid table decorations they managed to come up with at the annual Halloween party."

Meredith sat down in the silence of her apartment and sipped her hot tea. She didn't know which she was enjoying more, the soothing warmth of the tea or the soothing silence that had settled in after the girls had left.

She usually liked the girls around, especially the three from 407, but she had never seen them like they had been today. Gigi Norton certainly brought out the worst in her girls. She was beginning to wish she had taken Patrice Allardyce's advice and just asked a few people to help with the party, instead of posting the notice in the student center.

But she had been hoping to interest some of the other students in helping with the Halloween party. It seemed like the same few volunteers ended up doing everything around there, and she wanted to give them a break and at the same time get to know some of the other girls.

Well, she was getting to know some of the other girls all right, and if Gigi Norton was typical of the girls in Addison, Meredith felt lucky to be the housemother at Baker.

CHAPTER THREE

Jane was seething as the five girls from Baker walked across the campus on the next Saturday morning. Her mind kept replaying all the digs Gigi had made at Cary and his band. Still, Gigi hadn't found anyone to replace Ambulance. Merry had finally said that since Gigi still hadn't come up with an alternative to Ambulance, and the party was next Saturday, it was best to go with what they had.

What they had! How dare Gigi make Cary's band sound like second choice? Ambulance was a good band, and they were just lucky that they would be able to play.

Gigi had sucked in her anger and said, "That's fine. Why doesn't Jane take care of that, while we concentrate on the haunted house? But be sure and tell the band that with so much to do, not many people will feel like dancing unless the music is really good this time."

Andy had placed a restraining hand gently on Jane's forearm before leaning forward and saying, "We'll do that. You just do your thing and we'll do ours."

"Well, now, that sounds like a great idea. Everyone doing her own job," Meredith said with artificial cheeriness.

"There's Cary," Toby said. Jane looked over and saw Cary sitting on the same bench Andy had sat on the day she saw the notice for the Halloween party. His slightly long, silky hair was being gently tossed by the breeze. Sitting by himself on the bench he looked so cute — and out of place — that Jane's heart went out to him.

"I'll see you guys later," Jane said as she cut diagonally across the lawn toward him. When Cary saw her, he stood up and waved.

Jane let herself be encircled in his strong arms. He lightly kissed her cheek. "How was the meeting?"

"Don't ask." Jane sat down on the bench. He sat beside her.

"That bad, huh?"

"I just don't know how anybody as rotten as Gigi Norton can stand to look at herself in the mirror every day. That's probably why she wears so much makeup. She can't stand to look at her own face."

Cary smiled. "Come on. Where is that Barrett of Boston spirit I've come to know and love? I can't believe anybody can get the best of you."

"Well, they can," Jane said, pulling away from him. Cary had felt like there was something different about their relationship this year. More accurately, it had seemed different ever since Jane went to Texas.

He couldn't put his finger on any one thing that was different. They didn't disagree any more than usual or see each other less. It was just that sometimes, he had a feeling she was somewhere else, especially when they talked about Toby or when something came up about Randy and his farm. Suddenly Jane would seem to just drift away for a few seconds. Then she'd snap out of it and be herself again.

At first he thought she might be falling for Randy Crowell, but Cary knew better than that. Randy was a good friend to the girls, but that's all it was. And besides, if Randy was going to fall for any of the girls from 407, it would have been Toby Houston. But Randy was almost twenty-one, and he wasn't romantically interested in any of the girls from Canby Hall.

Cary stood up and took Jane by the hand. "Come on. Let's go into Greenleaf and get a pizza. What do you say?"

Jane turned her warm smile on him and

said, "I say that sounds great." Jane promised herself she would just put the whole
meeting out of her mind. Cary had agreed
to play for the dance, and the band was
looking forward to it.

As if Cary had read her mind, he said,
"The guys are really excited about the dance
next week." The boys in the band all went
to Oakley Prep, which was a boys' school
down the road. Ambulance liked playing
for the Canby Hall girls. On break there
were lots of girls to talk to the band members
and admire their music. All that attention
was great. "Believe me, there's probably
nothing Gigi Norton could do to ruin it."

"I wouldn't be so sure if I were you."

They sat down in front of a great-looking
pepperoni pizza. The tantalizing smell
teased their senses with mouth-watering
promises of good taste.

Jane looked across the table at Cary, who
had taken a generous bite of the hot pizza
and was sucking in little mouthfuls of air to
cool off. He drained his glass of Coke and
refilled it from the pitcher on the table.

"Hot?" Jane asked. She laughed at him
and took a much smaller and more cautious
bite of the piece in her hand. Even so, the
hot cheese stung the roof of her mouth.

Through watery eyes, she saw the blurred
image of Gigi Norton coming up behind

Cary. "Hi, Jane," she said. "Oh, this must be your little friend from the band." Cary looked at Jane. Gigi tapped him on the shoulder and he turned around. "Hi, I'm Gigi Norton."

"I thought you might be," Cary said. Knowing him as well as she did, Jane detected the sarcasm in his voice. But if Gigi heard it, she went right on like she hadn't.

"We're so excited you're going to be playing for us at the dance next Saturday."

Jane nearly choked on her pizza. She hadn't said anything specific to Cary about Gigi's cruel put-downs. After all, it had all worked out. Why hurt Cary's feelings unnecessarily?

Then Gigi pushed her way into the booth next to Cary. "I really like your voice. It's a shame not all the band is as good as you.

"I think they're pretty good," Cary said defensively as he took another slice.

"Of course they are," Gigi said quickly. "But they're just not as good as you are, and it seems like they sort of drag you down. You know, lots of famous singers had to give up their little amateur bands when they hit the big time. Guys like Buddy Holly and Ritchie Valens."

She leaned over and took a piece of pepperoni off Cary's pizza. Jane didn't know who was more startled, she or Cary. "You know, I saw that movie about Ritchie Valens and I just cried. Can you imagine being dead at seventeen?"

Jane watched Gigi lean into her boyfriend and flirt with him like Jane didn't even exist, and she could very easily imagine Gigi being dead at *sixteen*.

"Uh. . . . Well, no, actually, I never really thought about it," Cary said.

"Well, silly me," Gigi said, getting up from the booth. "Here you are trying to have a nice little romantic lunch, and I just busted right in and ruined everything."

"Don't flatter yourself, Gigi," Jane said coolly, "We'll get over it." Gigi flashed them her best phony smile and went over to order her own pizza.

"So that's the infamous Gigi Norton?" Cary said after she walked away. "She didn't seem that bad to me." He took another slice of pizza from the tray.

Wordlessly, Jane reached for her Coke. She accidentally knocked the glass over onto the pizza.

"Hey, take it easy," Cary said, grabbing some napkins to mop up. "I didn't say she was the greatest or anything, I just said she wasn't that bad."

"Well, you wouldn't think so if you had to room with her for a year and watch her scheming and conniving to manipulate people. She's very good at that. Especially with boys," Jane said pointedly.

"Cool down," Cary said. "What are you getting so steamed about? She's not my type."

"She isn't?" Jane asked softly.

"No, I like girls with blonde hair and a face I can see, that isn't hidden behind a lot of makeup. Girls kind of like you, I guess." His smile broadened and he stood up. "Come on. Let's get out of here."

Jane looked at the soggy half a pizza that was swimming in Coke on the table. "I'm sorry about the pizza."

"Forget it, I was almost full anyway." He put his arm around Jane.

From a table near the back, Gigi watched the two of them walk out the door. How had that stuffy Jane Barrett managed to snag someone that good-looking? Well, it wouldn't matter for long because if *she* had anything to do with it, Jane wouldn't be keeping him.

At dinner, the barbecued beef sandwich in front of Jane remained untouched as she sat near the large window in the dining hall telling her roommates about Gigi's performance at Pizza Pete's. "And she sat right down beside him like they were best friends?" Andy asked. "Can you believe the nerve?"

"She says all that stuff about how rotten the band is in front of all of us at Merry's," said Toby, "and then she sits there and tells him how great she thinks he is."

"That's about as two-faced as they come," Andy seethed.

"Well, we've always known that about her," Toby said. "I don't know why anything she does should surprise us."

"Speaking of surprises, I wonder what she's got cooked up for us in that haunted house she and Yolanda are planning."

"It's almost too scary to think about," Jane said with a shudder.

"It's no wonder you're shivering, little lady," a familiar voice said from over her shoulder. "You don't eat enough to keep a bird alive."

Jane knew that voice! It was Beau Stockton's, the boy she had met last summer at Toby's place out in Texas! But what was he doing in Boston? She spun around to see if her ears were playing tricks on her.

There standing beside her was Beau, tall and lanky, with rugged good looks that were almost breath-taking. He threw his booted foot over the chair next to hers and easily slid down beside her. "This seat taken, Boston?" he said as he sat down.

"*Beau*? What are you doing here?" Jane asked.

"Yeah," Toby echoed, "What *are* you doing here?" Beau was a senior at Rio Verde High School in Texas, and that was a long way from Greenleaf, Massachusetts.

"Well, I had to leave on account of an illness," Beau said running his hand through his soft brown curls.

"An illness?" Jane asked with concern. "What's wrong?"

"It's my heart," Beau said, shaking his head sadly.

"Your heart?" Jane said as sick dread spread through her. All sorts of frightening things ran through her mind. She thought about movies she'd seen where kids got cancer or heart disease and died. She thought about what Gigi had said to Cary earlier that afternoon about dying when you're only seventeen. Jane looked at his tanned face and his twinkling green eyes. Sitting beside her in the light of sunset, Beau looked the picture of health. He couldn't be sick. Could he?

"Yep," he said, leaning back in the chair, enjoying all the attention he was getting from the three of them. "I was walking across campus one afternoon just minding my own business, and I saw this girl with long blonde hair off in the distance and that's when it happened. I got this pain in my chest and my heart just started to ache. Rather than pine away and die, it seemed a whole lot easier for me to hop a plane and get a dose of you so I could go on with life." His face broke into a wide grin that moved up to his eyes and set them sparkling as he started to laugh.

His laughter echoed through the dining hall and caught the attention of Gigi Norton. She elbowed Yolanda and said, "Who's that guy with Jane Barrett over there?"

"I've never seen him before," Yolanda said, straining to get a better look. "But from here, he sure does look fine."

"Well, isn't this interesting?" Gigi said as she picked up her tray and started toward Jane's table. "It looks like Ms. Barrett has found herself a new boyfriend. I wonder what her rock singer would think about all this?"

Yolanda grabbed her own tray and hurried after Gigi. They put them on the return cart and walked right by Jane's table.

"Hi, Jane," Gigi said. "I really enjoyed meeting your boyfriend today." Then she stopped and put her hand dramatically to her lips. "Oh, my gosh, I didn't see you sitting here. Are you a friend of Jane's?"

Beau nodded. Then he said, "But obviously, you aren't."

"Well, maybe not anymore. Me and my big mouth. Sorry, Jane," Gigi said. "I hope I didn't say anything wrong."

"Yeah, I'll just bet," Andy said.

CHAPTER FOUR

Gigi and Yolanda walked out of the now nearly deserted cafeteria, leaving Andy, Toby, Jane, and Beau sitting in uncomfortable silence. The sounds of the dining hall staff clearing and washing the tables were the only noises in the big room.

Beau leaned back and stretched dramatically. "Well, I sure could use a place to lay my head down. I don't imagine they got visitors quarters in the dorm, huh?"

"Not for males anyway," Andy said.

"Then how about a hotel? They got one of those anywhere around here? Of course, it don't matter, I can throw a sleeping bag down any old place and be happy."

"You don't have to sleep on the ground," Jane reassured him. "There's the Greenleaf Inn in town."

"I've got a better idea," Toby said.

"What's that?" Beau asked.

"Where's your stuff?"

"That duffel bag by the door is all I brought."

"Then grab it and follow me," Toby said, getting to her feet.

Jane and Andy got up, too. All three girls dumped their trays off and followed Toby. "Where are we going?" Jane asked.

"Randy's."

"Randy's?" Beau asked. Who was this Randy guy? Surely he wasn't the boyfriend that that black-haired girl was talking about. But there was no telling with that October Houston. She might just pull anything. Of course, he'd pulled a few things on her himself back home. Maybe this was her shot at getting even.

As they came out of the dining hall, the sun was just setting. It was getting much colder than it had been during the day. Beau rubbed the arms of his cotton shirt vigorously. "Feels like we're in for some cool weather, ladies."

Jane looked at the down vest he wore and said, "Well, if you had sleeves in your jacket, it would be much warmer."

"Little lady, for your information, this vest is plenty warm in Texas. Now for my information, who is this Randy?"

"He's a friend of ours," Jane said. "Well, mostly of Toby's. Their place is just down the road from Canby Hall." They were crossing the orchard, which was now filled with bare trees whose empty black branches reached up to the darkening sky like eerie fingers of some long, wicked hand. Jane moved over closer to Beau.

After a short walk they came to the white gate that marked the entrance to the Crowell farm. Toby opened the gate. "Well, here we are."

Beau saw an old New England two-story farmhouse looming in the distance. The lighted windows looked like welcome beacons in a storm. He wondered how these people might feel about taking in a stranger, but if they were anything like the farmers and ranchers back in Texas, they would think nothing of it.

Toby knocked at the back door, and a slightly plump lady with reddish-brown hair answered her knock. She was wiping her hands on an apron, and her face lit up when she saw Toby. "Well, well, what are you doing out here this time of night? It's too dark to go riding."

Beau figured that this must be Randy's mom. She opened the door wider and saw the other three standing in the shadows of the back porch. "Come on in. Don't stand out there in the cold. We're just finishing dinner. You got here just in time for desert."

"Oh, we don't want to intrude," Andy said as she came up the back steps.

"It's apple cobbler with vanilla ice cream," she said.

"Well, we might intrude a little," Toby said.

"Then come on in. Who's your friend?"

"Oh, Ms. Crowell, this is Beau Stockton. His folks have the ranch next to ours back in Rio Verde."

"Rio Verde? Are you another one of those Texas kids who got lost?"

"No, ma'am, I'm just visiting for a few days. I can always find my way back to Texas."

Randy pushed his chair back from the table and stood up. "Hey, Tobe, what brings you this way on a chilly Saturday evening?"

"Actually, he does." She nodded toward Beau. "Beau Stockton, this is Randy Crowell and his father." They all shook hands.

"Sit down," Randy said, sliding his chair over to make room at the big old oak table.

Randy's mom started handing out dessert to everyone. It smelled delicious, particularly after the food at Canby Hall, which was enough to get anyone to stop eating.

As Ms. Crowell set a bowl in front of Jane, Beau reached out and took it away. "Ah, ah, ah," he said shaking his head. "She didn't finish her dinner. I'm not sure she ought to have dessert."

For a stunned moment, the Crowells stared at Beau, not sure whether to take him seriously or not. Then Jane playfully slapped at his arm and took the bowl back from him.

While they ate, Randy kept up a steady stream of questions about ranching in Texas, which Beau was more than happy to answer. Watching the two of them, Jane marveled at how easily they got along with one another. It was as if they'd known each other for ages. But then why shouldn't they hit it off? They both dressed the same — in jeans and boots and western shirts. They both grew up on ranches. And they both loved riding horses. It shouldn't surprise her that Randy and Beau would like each other; what was so surprising was that *she* and Beau should like each other.

"So, how long are you here for?" Randy asked.

"A week."

"I hope you can stay for the Halloween party next Saturday night," Andy said. Jane kicked her under the table. If Beau stayed for the Halloween party, at which Cary was playing, they were sure to run into each other. But if Beau left on Saturday afternoon and she kept him safely hidden away at Randy's, she might be able to keep Beau and Cary from meeting.

Beau already knew that she was seeing someone else because he had asked her about it last summer, and if he'd forgotten about it, Gigi had reminded him earlier. But Cary had no idea that she'd met anyone in Texas, and Jane thought it would be better if he didn't find out.

"I should be able to make that," Beau said. "My plane doesn't leave till Sunday."

"Where you staying?" Randy asked. "You're not at the Greenleaf Inn, are you?"

"Well, no . . . he's uh — " Toby said.

"Good, because the food's okay, but it's much better here and we got all kinds of extra room, don't we, Mom?"

Ms. Crowell smiled and nodded in agreement. "And besides, you'd be closer to the school."

"What a great idea," Toby said with relief. She knew it would be okay with the Crowells for Beau to stay there, but she hadn't been sure how she could go about asking them. If it had just been her and Randy that would have been no problem, but with his parents sitting there and Beau waiting for an answer, it would have been really embarrassing if they'd have had to turn him down.

"Well, that's settled then," Ms. Crowell said, gathering the dishes. "Anyone want a second helping?"

"We'd better be getting back to the dorm," Toby said. She got up and carried her dish to the sink. "Thanks for dessert, Ms. Crowell."

"You're welcome anytime, Toby." She hugged her warmly.

"Be careful what you say," Andy warned. "Toby just might take you up on that, and she has a good appetite."

"I'll walk you back to the school," Beau said, helping Jane with her jacket.

"We'll go on and meet you back in the room," Andy said, giving Toby a shove out the door.

Darkness had settled in when they left the Crowells'. Beau put his arm around Jane and pulled her close. She thought back to last summer when Andy had gotten lost and they'd gone looking for her that night. She felt so safe when she was with him. If she had been a pioneer, she would have wanted Beau Stockton by her side.

Thinking about being a pioneer woman without running water and indoor plumbing, she shuddered. "You cold?" Beau asked and held her even tighter.

They hopped the fence and walked beneath the dead branches of the orchard. The moonlight was casting weird shadows. She thought of Halloween and that got her to thinking about the Halloween party. She had to tell Beau about Cary. It wasn't like he didn't already know, but if one of them were to be prepared, it might be easier.

At the edge of the orchard, Jane stopped

and turned to him. "Beau, there's something I want to tell you."

He put his hands on her shoulders. "I know. You missed me, too, and you're glad I'm here." He leaned down and kissed her. The warmth of his lips melted her resolve to tell him about Cary. She got lost in his embrace. Her knees actually felt weak.

She would tell him about Cary another time. After all, Beau would be here all week. She would have plenty of time to bring it up before the party. Right now, she was contented in feeling like they were the only two people in the world.

Jane came into the room to find Andy sitting at her desk, sketching something and Toby lying across her bed, her leg crossed over one knee and a literature book propped up for reading.

"Quite a surprise, huh?" Toby asked looking up from her book.

"Yeah. What a surprise."

"I got a feeling," Andy said, "that Jane isn't the only one who's going to be surprised."

"You mean Cary?" Jane sank to her bed. "What am I going to do? Beau came all this way to see me, and I don't want to hurt his feelings. And Cary doesn't even know that Beau exists, so I can't very well introduce the two of them."

"Well, I have a feeling if Gigi Norton has anything to do with it, he'll know about Beau's existence before too much longer."

"That's what I'm afraid of. Oh, this would have been so much easier if Beau would have just settled for letters and phone calls."

Toby set her book on the bed and sat up. "You mean it would have been easy for you to go right on having your cake and eating it, too. But not really fair to Beau and Cary, don't you think?"

"Hey, I told Beau that I had a boyfriend when he asked me last summer."

"And did you tell Cary that you met a guy at Toby's?"

"No, why should I? I sure didn't expect him to just show up here one day."

"Well, he has," Toby said, "And if I were you, I'd start figuring out what I was going to say to Cary before Gigi beats you to it." She lay back down and resumed her reading.

"What am I going to do?" Jane wailed again.

"Well, one thing you could do is get over here and help me with this floorplan," Andy said.

"For what?"

"In case you've forgotten, we're supposed to be the decorating committee for the Halloween party. And you, my friend, are the chairperson."

"Oh, Andy, I haven't got time for that right now." Jane tossed the crumpled clothes that had been lying across her bed onto the chair, already overloaded with discards, and flopped onto the bed.

"Well, you'd better make time real soon, because the party is next week." Andy crumpled up the paper she had been working on and shot it across the room. It hit the rim of the garbage can and bounced in.

"Two points," Toby said, leaning around her book and winking at Andy.

"I will think about it," Jane promised. "Tomorrow." She pulled a pillow over her head and dreaded the thought of the sun coming up in the morning.

CHAPTER FIVE

Andy sat in the middle of her usually neat bed with tissue paper and Kleenex and Tootsie Pops spread all around her. The white end of a lollipop stick protruded from her mouth while she concentrated on the little Kleenex ghosts she was making.

Toby pushed the door open and stood in the doorway watching Andy, who was unaware of her presence. Looking at the heaps of tissue, Toby couldn't stand it any longer and laughed out loud, causing Andy to look up abruptly.

Andy pulled the Tootsie Pop from her mouth. "You nearly gave me a heart attack. What's the idea of sneaking up on me like that?"

"I didn't sneak up on you. The door was open, and besides, I live here, too. Remember?" Toby came over and sat on the chair beside Andy's bed. "What are you doing?"

"I saw these in a magazine. Aren't they cute?" She held up a Tootsie Pop wrapped in a tissue and tied with a string to resemble a ghost. She had drawn two black dots for eyes.

"What are they for?" Toby asked casually reaching over and picking up a chocolate pop for herself from under Andy's knee.

"They're to hang from the ceiling at the dance. Won't they be cute?"

"Sure if you can keep the guests from eating them, they'll be great." Toby got up and went to her own side of the room, which was fairly bare in comparison to Jane's usual clutter of dirty clothes and Andy's arrangement of posters and books.

"Why don't you help me with these?" Andy asked. "I need about one hundred of them to create the effect I want."

"A hundred?" Toby asked. "What effect are you going for? Winter wonderland? With all those tissues hanging from the ceiling, it'll look like a blizzard."

"Fine, I'll do it myself." Andy grabbed another Tootsie Pop and began folding the Kleenex around it.

Toby watched Andy's deep concentration as she worked at tying the string around the bottom of the sucker. Toby decided it didn't look like she was in for much excitement around here. It was a great day. Maybe she'd go over to Randy's and ride Maxine.

"See you later," she said as she walked past Andy's bed. Andy barely nodded as Toby left.

When Toby jumped the fence to the Crowells' place, she saw Beau and Jane sitting on the fence near the corral. She walked over to them. "What's up?"

"Howdy, October," Beau said.

"Beauregard," Toby answered. It was kind of a thing they did. Ever since she could remember, he had insisted on calling her by her full name, and she retaliated by calling him by his.

Randy came out of the barn and came over to the fence. "Hi, Toby. I hope you came out to ride. Maxine just told me she was hoping you'd stop by today."

Toby laughed and jumped off the fence. She followed Randy into the barn where Maxine whinnied at the sound of her voice. Though she knew Maxine hadn't *really* asked about her, she believed that horses could communicate with people, and Maxine probably *had* been wishing Toby would stop by today.

"You want to go riding, too?" Jane asked Beau as he watched Randy and Toby go into the barn.

"Nope," Beau said. "I can ride anytime. I've only got a few days to be with you." He jumped off the fence and held his hands up to her and lifted her down beside him. "Why don't you take me on a tour of Canby Hall?"

As they walked through the autumn leaves crunching beneath their feet, Jane pointed out various buildings around Canby Hall. The large home that faced the park belonged to Patrice Allardyce. "She's the headmistress. If you look up *strict* in the dictionary, there's a picture of P.A."

"That's good to know," Beau said, "because otherwise I might break some rules!"

They crossed the park and stopped in front of a shallow cement pond.

"This is the wishing pool." Jane sat down on a bench and looked at the clear water with the few coins scattered in the bottom. Big golden carp were swimming lazily back and forth.

Beau took some change from his pocket and tossed it in the pool. He handed her a quarter. "Your turn." Jane closed her eyes and made a wish before tossing the quarter to the center of the pool. "What'd you wish for?"

"If I tell you, it won't come true," Jane said.

They walked on past the main building and the library toward the student center. Jane pointed out Addison House and Charles House as they went by.

They went toward Baker House and sat

on the steps watching a group of girls play Frisbee on the lawn. "Looks like you have a lot of fun here," Beau said. "It isn't so much different from Rio Verde High, really, except it's all girls."

"I don't think you'd have any trouble with that part," Jane said.

"The only girl I want is sitting right beside me." Beau put his arm around her and pulled her to him. She lay her head against his shoulder and looked up just in time to see Cary's red car pull up to the curb. Her heart seemed to come to a complete stop before racing off at ninety miles an hour.

She sat upright and pulled away from Beau. It couldn't be! Why would Cary come by without calling her? Her mind was racing as quickly as her heart. Should she grab Beau's hand and run off? Should she run off and leave Beau sitting there alone to face Cary? Should she just go to the wishing pool and jump in?

Cary had been working on an English paper so long his eyes felt crossed. He had finally decided to toss it aside and take a break. He'd gotten into his car and suddenly wanted to see Jane very much. So he had taken the chance that she wasn't busy with the Halloween party committee and would be able to see a movie or at least grab something to eat.

When Cary pulled up, he was sure he'd

seen a couple sitting on the steps of Baker, wrapped in each other's arms. That wouldn't be that unusual, but for a minute, he thought the girl looked like Jane. As he got out of the car and crossed the lawn, he began to realize the girl *was* Jane and the guy looked like Randy Crowell. Jane had probably been upset about something Gigi Norton had done and Randy was comforting her. He was kind of the honorary big brother of 407. Cary waved to them.

Beau saw a strange-looking kid, badly in need of a haircut, coming toward them. When he raised his hand to wave, Beau looked around to see who he was waving at. Other than the girls playing Frisbee on the lawn, there wasn't anyone else around. No one seemed to be waving back.

Then Jane raised her own arm and waved back to him. Beau stepped away from her in disbelief. "You know that New Age hippie?"

Jane felt her temper flare. "You have a lot of nerve calling him names. You don't even know him."

"I know he needs a haircut. Who is he, anyway?"

"His name is Cary Slade. He goes to Oakley Prep. It's about a half a mile from here."

"Well, isn't that convenient!"

Cary reached the steps and Jane drew a

deep breath and prepared for what might easily become the worst moment of her life. "Hi, there," Cary said.

"Hi, Cary." Jane stopped, but both boys were looking at each other and she couldn't very well pretend they didn't exist. "Um, Cary . . . this is a friend of Toby's. He's from Texas. I met him this summer when we were out there. Beau Stockton, this is Cary Slade. Cary, this is Beau."

Cary moved onto the porch next to them and reached out to take Beau's outstretched hand. At the same time that he put his other arm around Jane's waist. Beau shook Cary's hand, all the while looking at Jane — the same girl *he* had been holding himself just a few minutes ago.

Could this be? No way. Jane couldn't possibly be interested in that guy? But still, there *was* someone else. She had told him so herself last summer, and then that girl in the cafeteria had mentioned a boyfriend. But this dweeb? Beau took a step backward and stared. Cary seemed unaware of Beau's gaze.

"So how long are you here for?"

Beau became aware that Cary was saying something to him. "What?"

"I said, how long are you here for? Did you come down especially to see Toby, or are you here on vacation?"

See Toby, huh? Well it was obvious that

Jane may have said something about having a boyfriend to Beau, but she sure hadn't said anything about Beau to Cary. So where did that leave him? He looked at the two of them standing together. Out in the cold, that's where. He'd sure spent a lot of money and come a long way to get frozen out.

He shook his head. He was such a green-horn sometimes! Back in Texas it had seemed like such a good idea to come out here. Now it just seemed stupid.

"Well, Boston, I can see how things are." Beau stopped and pulled the collar of his jean jacket up around his neck against the breeze that had picked up in the last few minutes. "But I gotta admit, I figured you more for the Harvard type, you know? You surprise me, Boston."

He jumped from the porch and started across the lawn, his hands burrowed deep into his pockets against the cold wind. He didn't run and he didn't look back. He just walked steadily away from them. Jane stood and watched him go, tears stinging her eyes. Darn him. Why had he come here in the first place? And why did she have to care at all?

Cary moved away from Jane. "What was that all about? Hey, are you crying?"

"No," Jane said. "That sudden gust of wind just caused my eyes to water for a minute." She took one last quick look at

Beau's figure off in the distance. Then she turned back to Cary.

"Jane, who is that guy really?"

"Well, he's . . . he's a neighbor of Toby's."

"Forget what he is to Toby. I want to know what he is to you."

"To me? He's a . . . a friend, that's all."

"A friend? And he came all the way out here from Texas? Come on, Jane. I'm not that stupid. No guy hauls himself all the way across the country to see 'just a friend'! There's more to it than that, isn't there?"

"Well, not like you think."

"What am I supposed to think? You came back from Texas, and you were a different person. The whole month after you got back, you were a million miles away. I figured something was wrong, I just never figured that you'd gone off to Texas and fallen in love with Billy the Kid."

Cary got to his feet and started toward the steps. "Wait," Jane called. "At least give me a minute to explain."

He stopped on the bottom step and looked up at her. "You had a lot of minutes to explain these past few months. I think it's a little late for that now." He pulled his car keys from his pocket and turned his back on her.

Jane sank onto the top step and let go with a tremendous sob. She should have told Cary about Beau. She should have told

Beau a lot more about Cary. Last summer when he had asked if there was someone else, she had nodded, but she had never said anything about who the someone was.

Face it, Jane Barrett, she said to herself, you wanted it all. And now here you sit with nothing. Nothing but a rotten feeling and a broken heart.

As she got to her feet she could see the wishing pond off in the distance. That was the last time she'd ever trust that thing. She had wished more than anything that Beau and Cary would never find out about each other, and it hadn't even worked for a day. She was glad she'd only invested a quarter.

CHAPTER
SIX

Jane came into the room so overwhelmed by her own feelings of despair she was oblivious to the mess that was strewn from one end to the other. She sighed deeply and sank onto her bed.

Andy was sitting cross-legged on the floor with a sketch pad in her lap, and she looked up when Jane sighed. "What's wrong?"

"What isn't?" Jane said. Then she started to cry again. The whole story about Beau and Cary's meeting came flooding out. Andy held the sketch pad up and rested her chin on top of it while she listened.

Jane paced around, stepping on discarded drawings beneath her feet while she picked up things around the room and tossed them into the air. "This is just awful," she wailed. "What am I going to do now?"

She reached over and took a balled-up Kleenex from Andy's bed and started to blow her nose. She stopped short when she nearly poked herself in the eye with the stick pointing out of the bottom of it. "What is this?"

"That's part of the decorations for the Halloween party Saturday night. Not that you'd care. You only happen to be the chairperson of the committee."

"Oh, Andy, you can't possibly think that I have time to worry about that now with everything else that's going on?"

"When do you expect to start worrying? Next Saturday night when Gigi Norton has this fantastic haunted house finished and we have nothing?"

Toby opened the door and stood in the doorway, looking at the chaos in 407. "What's going on here? I heard you yelling all the way down the hall."

"Nothing you'd care about," Andy said. She struggled to get to her feet. "In fact, I don't think either of you cares much what happens at that party next week. I don't know why you ever bothered to volunteer for the committee in the first place."

"Hey, wait a minute," Toby said. "I don't mind being on the committee and decorating the student center next Saturday, but I sure don't plan to spend the next week locked up in this room making ghosts out of Kleenex and Tootsie Pops."

"You don't have to. They're all done."

Andy grabbed her jacket from the back of the chair. "I'm going over to the student center."

"You want us to come with you?" Toby asked.

"No. I can go alone. I'm getting used to it." Andy brushed past Toby on her way out. Toby picked up the brown paper sack from the floor and began putting the Kleenex ghosts into the bag.

"I don't know why she's acting like that," Jane sniffed.

"Well, we did agree to be on the committee. If we didn't want to do it, we should have said no." Toby picked up the last of the ghosts and put them in the bag.

"If I remember right, we did."

"But then we said we'd do it, and we haven't done a thing. It's only for a week. And how much more can there be left to do?" Toby put the bag on the top shelf in the closet.

"A week? My whole life could fall apart in the next week, and you guys actually expect me to be able to think about decorations for some Halloween party?"

"Do what you want," Toby said, opening the door. "I just know that from now on, I'm going to be helping Andy."

Andy went into the busy student center. It was Sunday night, and a lot of the girls came over to get snacks from the vending machines and cluster around the big-screen TV to watch *Sixty Minutes*.

Andy went over to the vending machines and studied the choices. Nothing much looked that good. She finally decided on some of the square cheese crackers that had peanut butter middles. She dropped her money in the slot and made her selection. Well, that was dinner. Now for desert. She looked at the candy bars behind the glass. Finally, she decided on a Baby Ruth.

"That's not very nutritious." Andy looked up and saw Toby's reflection behind hers in the glass. She turned around.

"Well, they don't exactly offer meat and potatoes in these things."

"If they did, it would put the dining hall out of business." Toby reached into her jeans, pulled out some change, and bought a bag of potato chips.

They got Cokes and sat at one of the tables. "I'm sorry we bugged out on you today," Toby said. "It won't happen again. You can count on me to do anything you need."

"It's okay. I probably overreacted. It's just that I know that Gigi will stop at nothing to make herself look good and us look bad. She's not above hiring some architect to come in and build that spook house just to show us up."

"I wouldn't worry about that. Gigi Norton may be a creep, but she's not crazy enough to spend that kind of money."

"Did I hear my name?" Gigi asked from over Toby's shoulder.

"I don't know, did you?" Toby said without turning around.

"Well, I've always had excellent hearing. . . ."

"Most dogs do," Toby said under her breath to Andy, who giggled.

"What?"

"I thought you had excellent hearing," Andy said.

"Well, how's the decoration committee doing?" Gigi asked. She was carefully unwrapping a peanut butter cup, pulling the brown paper wrapper delicately away from the chocolate candy.

"We're doing fine. How's the haunted house committee?"

"Just great," Gigi said with a sunny smile. "In fact, it's coming along so well, it's scary." Yolanda laughed. "Well, we have to get back to work," Gigi said. "We just stopped in for some quick energy." She took a dainty bite from the candy in her hand.

"Good-*bye*," Andy said.

Toby watched Gigi and Yolanda weave through the tables toward the door. "Come on," Toby said as she gathered her garbage and got to her feet.

"Where we going?"

"Back to Baker. We've got a lot to do before next week."

Toby and Andy sat in the middle of Maggie and Dee's room discussing the centerpieces for the table. They had decided on carving pumpkins for each table, which in itself wasn't very original, but with Dee's artistic talents, each one promised to be unique.

As they worked, Andy filled the girls in on Jane's situation. They all agreed that it might be best to leave Jane alone for tonight. There would be plenty for her to do tomorrow.

There was a knock at the door. "Hey, Houston," one of the girls said, sticking her head in, "you got a phone call in your room. Jane said you might be in here."

"Thanks." Toby got to her feet and went to her room. Jane had left, but the phone was lying beside the receiver. Toby picked up the phone. "Hello."

"It took you long enough. This is long distance, you know." The voice on the other end belonged to Cornelius Worthington III, better known as Neal. He was a good friend of Jane's, in fact, a sort of boyfriend, until Jane had met Cary. Now Toby and Neal had a special friendship.

"Neal," Toby said. "It's great to hear your voice. What's up?"

"Nothing. I just got to thinking about you, and I felt like talking to you. What's up with you?"

"Not much. We're working on the decorations for the Halloween party for next Saturday."

"Party?" Neal asked with interest.

"Yeah. Hey, I've got a great idea! Why don't you come down? It should be lots of fun." Even as she spoke, Toby marveled at how easy that had been. The first time she had asked him to a party, it was the Winter Blahs party Jane and Andy had given her last winter, and she had nearly died of embarrassment. It had taken every bit of nerve to call and ask him. This time she hadn't even had to think about it.

"I'd love to. I was hoping to see you again. This will be a great excuse to come to Greenleaf." They talked about the party for a while. Toby told him about the costumes and what to expect when he got there. Then she said, "And there's something else you should expect when you get here."

"What's that?"

"Jane met this guy when she was in Texas last summer, and he sort of took her by surprise when he showed up here yesterday."

"I'll bet she was surprised."

"Well, I guess she wasn't nearly as surprised as Cary was when they ran into each other today."

"I can imagine. It wasn't so long ago that Cary was the other guy, and I was the one getting the shaft."

Neal and Jane had been dating since they were in junior high. Then, out of the blue, Jane met Cary at a dance and much to the surprise of everyone, including herself, they had begun dating. Neal had to admit, now that it was over, he had gotten over it just fine. In fact, he was glad things had worked out like they had, because otherwise he would have never gotten to know Toby. And the more he knew of Toby, the more he liked her. She was so different from the girls he had known before.

"Hey," he said, "don't get the idea that I still care about Jane. I mean, I *do* care about her, but only as her friend. I'd be a lot more upset if this guy had come all the way from Texas to see you instead."

Toby felt her face growing hot, and knew she was turning as red as her hair. She was grateful that video phones never caught on. She was still new at the idea of boyfriends, but she had to admit, there was something very nice about knowing Neal cared whether or not another guy paid attention to her.

They talked a while longer before they hung up. Toby put the receiver back and stared at the phone, lost in her thoughts of seeing Neal next weekend.

Andy came in from Maggie and Dee's room. "Who was that?" Toby turned around to look in Andy's direction. "Never mind. I can tell by that look on your face, it must have been Neal. What did he have to say?"

"Nothing much. He just called to say hi, and I invited him to the Halloween party next week."

"Is he coming?" Andy asked.

"Yes! And we have to make this the best party ever. If Neal is coming all the way from Boston, I don't want him spending all night in the haunted house. I can think of better ways for us to spend some time."

"I wish Matt didn't have that wedding to go to next weekend," Andy sighed.

The girls looked up as Jane came back in.

"Did you get your phone call?" she asked. Toby nodded.

"How's Neal doing?" Jane's face brightened, and she seemed to forget about her own boy troubles for a minute. "What did he have to say?"

"Nothing much, except that he missed me, and he's coming down for the Halloween party next week!" Toby fairly screamed the last part of the sentence. Jane jumped to her feet, and the three girls hugged each other and danced in a circle.

"I wish Matt could be here next week. This is going to be so much fun," Andy said. "I can hardly wait."

Jane dropped her arms and sat back on her bed. "I can. I don't even want to think about what will happen if Beau shows up while Cary's playing. Oh, why doesn't his plane leave Saturday morning?" Jane sighed.

"Look, you've got all week to work things out with the two of them. You can talk to Beau in the morning," Andy said.

"Oh, Toby, what will I say to him?" Jane asked Toby, who had retreated to her own bed.

"Don't ask me. What are you asking me for? I'm not an expert on the opposite sex."

"No, but you grew up next door to Beau; you ought to be some kind of expert on him!"

"The Beau I knew isn't the same guy as the one who would drop everything and come flying out here on a whim. I didn't even think he was aware of the opposite sex, let alone attracted to it."

"Maybe he's a late bloomer," Jane said. "Or maybe it's just something in the water in Rio Verde. If I remember right, you weren't overly fond of the opposite sex either before you met Neal."

"Look, Jane, all you have to do is decide which guy you'd rather be with next week and try to explain it to the other one," Andy said, sitting on the bed next to her roommate.

"But I can't do that. I've been sitting up here ever since Beau and Cary left, trying to figure out which one I should call and make up with, but I couldn't decide. I like them both. Why should I have to make a choice between them? I'm not planning to get married or anything. I don't know why they can't get along and make this a good week for everybody."

"Don't you mean a good week for you?" Andy asked. "It would be nice if Beau and Cary could get along great, and you could spend the night dancing away like it was *American Bandstand*. But, I think, you'd better start preparing yourself for something more like *All-Star Wrestling*!"

CHAPTER SEVEN

Jane rolled over and opened one eye, looking at the clock near the bed. She had heard Andy and Toby get up a while before. They had probably gone to breakfast. That was nothing new. Jane had always preferred sleeping late to eating early.

It was almost seven-fifteen. She had to pull herself out of bed to get ready for her first class. She moaned and pulled the pillow back over her head. How was she going to concentrate on class when she had so much more on her mind? She just wanted to pull the covers up and stay in bed for the next week. By then the Halloween party would be over, and Beau would be on his way back to Texas. But she couldn't stay in bed for a week any more than she could dodge Cary and Beau. She had to get up and face things.

All the while she was getting dressed, she

thought about what she was going to do. In fact, she had spent most of the night before tossing and turning and thinking about it. She was still just as confused as ever.

Jane came out of Baker House to a pleasantly warm morning for mid-fall. The early sunshine and the clear blue sky put a positive perspective on things. She had almost decided she could work the situation out.

Jane heard someone call her name and stopped. She thought it might be Andy and Toby. She turned around and spotted Gigi's black mop of hair. She was waving at Jane. Jane looked back over her shoulder to be sure Gigi was waving at her. There was no one else around.

"Hi, Jane. Where's your friend? That cute guy you were with Saturday?"

"What cute guy?"

"Oh, that's right. You were with two of them, weren't you? The one that's playing for the dance. I just needed to ask him something about Saturday night."

"What about it?" Jane asked suspiciously.

"Just something about the dance. I know he goes to Oakley Prep, and I wanted to get some names from him of guys who might be willing to help out with the haunted house."

"Why?"

"You certainly are curious this morning.

It's a surprise. You'll find out Saturday. Would you mind giving me his phone number?"

"Look, Gigi, if you want to call him up so you can let it slip that Beau's in town, you're too late. He already knows." Jane started to walk away.

"Why, you mean he. . . . Oh, he didn't know about that guy from Texas? Gee, I hope it didn't cause any problems."

"Nothing I can't handle." Jane was walking toward first period with Gigi right beside her.

"Well, anyway, I still need Cary's number so I can call him about the dance."

"You'll have to look it up. He always calls me," Jane said. Which, of course, wasn't true. She knew Cary's number as well as she knew her own, but she wasn't about to give it to Gigi Norton. "I've got to hurry. I'm going to be late to first period."

Gigi watched Jane go. A smile crept across her face. So, there was trouble. Looked like Lady Jane had one boy too many these days. Well, Gigi could help her out. Cary wasn't exactly her type, but he wasn't all that bad to look at, either. And if Jane was preoccupied with her cowboy, Cary might be looking to get even. That would make him an easy conquest. Yes, this Halloween party was getting more and more interesting!

* * *

Jane came out of her last class relieved she was finished for the day. It had been impossible to concentrate. She had almost left right after lunch and gone over to the Crowell place. She had to talk to Beau. She hurried back to the room to change clothes and go to Randy's.

Jane had just finished pulling her sweatshirt on when Toby opened the door. "I looked for you after class. Where did you disappear to so fast?"

"I thought I'd try to talk things out with Beau."

"I think that's a good idea. After all, he did come a long way to see you."

"I know. I'm still not sure if I should be talking to him or to Cary, but I have to start somewhere and Beau's closer. And besides, I have a lot longer to make up with Cary. After this week, Beau will be back in Texas, and it'll be harder to talk to him."

Jane's resolve began to melt a little when she got closer to the Crowell place. What if Beau wouldn't talk to her? What if he had already gone back to Texas? For just a split second, she felt a tinge of relief. What if he had? That would solve all her problems.

Then she saw Randy and Beau coming out of the barn together. They were laughing at something, and Beau didn't look like a man nursing a broken heart. Beau looked up and saw her near the fence. He came over to her and put his foot on the bottom rung, and leaned on the top rail with his hands crossed loosely in front of him.

"Wondered if I'd see you today," he said in his casual way.

"I had to go to classes. I was hoping maybe we could talk." Jane pulled herself up onto the fence and hopped down on the other side.

"That's good," he said as he turned around and leaned against the fence. " 'Cause I was kind of hoping the same thing. But, ladies first."

Jane looked over at him. He had his arms crossed in front of his chest and a hint of a smile played at the corner of his lips. Oh, why did he have to be so darned good-looking?

"I just wanted to tell you that I'm sorry about yesterday. I didn't know what to say. It all happened so fast. I didn't mean to hurt you."

"Whoa there, you didn't do any permanent damage. I'm tough. I spring back pretty quick. You ought to know that from last summer." Jane remembered when he had been tossed by a bull and knocked out for a minute. She had been sure the bull had killed him. Even after he walked out of the ring, she was afraid he wouldn't be able to come to the barn dance that night, and yet he had been there, and they had danced and talked all night.

"And there's something else you should know," he said turning to look at her. "I don't give up easy. Heck, I knew there had to be somebody else. Even if you hadn't kind of said something last summer, I would have figured it out. I didn't expect a girl like you to be unattached. But I don't care. And I just might be the one to get you to change your mind about what's-his-name. After all, you're here, aren't you?"

"I don't know, Beau. I want to see you while you're here, but I feel so bad for Cary. I — "

"Hey, it's my turn. He's got you all to himself for the rest of the year. I've only got one week. At least let me have that much, Boston."

He stepped toward her and touched her long blonde hair with the tip of his finger. His lips gently brushed her own. Jane folded into his arms and decided Cary would have to wait. At least for a week.

Gigi Norton tapped her foot impatiently as she waited to hear Cary's voice on the other end of the phone. She had called his dorm three times during the day and he had been out. Someone had finally told her to wait until later tonight and she might be able to catch him. She had done just that and now he was finally going to come to the phone.

She heard the noise on the other end of the phone as someone picked up the receiver.

Cary just knew it would be Jane on the phone. Some of the guys had told him that a girl had been calling him all afternoon. When she had called earlier, right before dinner, he had had them tell her he was still out. Let her sweat a little. She deserved it. Cary picked up the phone. "Hello."

"Hi, Cary." Cary's mind registered confusion for a minute. He had been so sure the voice would be Jane's that he was unable to recognize the person on the other end of the phone.

"This is Gigi Norton. You remember me from the other day at the pizza place?"

Now it was coming back to him. The girl he'd met Saturday with the thick black hair and too much makeup. How could he forget? "Yeah, what can I do for you?"

"Well, I got your number from Jane. I need a favor and she's just so busy with her friend from Texas and all, that I told her I'd call you."

"Her friend?"

"Yes. You know. The one who got here last weekend. She said you knew all about him. You do, don't you? I'd feel just awful if I was saying something I shouldn't."

"It's okay. I know about him. What's the favor?" he asked coldly. Gigi wasn't sure if his anger was directed at her for mentioning that other guy or at Jane, but she certainly hoped it was all for Jane.

"Well, I'm in charge of the haunted house, and we really need some guys to help us out with a few things, and since you know more guys than I do, I thought maybe you could help me out with some names."

"Sure. What do you need them to do?" he asked mechanically. Actually, he could care less about that stupid Halloween party now. He could just see himself up on the stage providing the background music so Jane and that hick could spend a romantic evening in each other's arms.

". . . And that's about all they'll need to do," Gigi was saying.

"I'm sorry. We must have a bad connection. I didn't hear that last part."

"I said, they'll just need to wear something creepy and grab people as they walk through. Maybe you could ask some of the guys who really like to goof around a lot and see if any of them would be interested."

"Yeah, I'll see what I can do."

"Thanks, Cary. I'll call you back in a couple days. Will that be okay?"

"Sure."

"And, Cary, thanks for your help. I won't forget it. I'm really looking forward to seeing you again."

"Yeah." Cary hung up the phone and

fought down his urge to punch the wall. So, Jane had been too busy to call him herself. Well, she sure had changed her tune since Saturday. At Pizza Pete's she didn't even want him so much as looking at Gigi Norton, and now Jane was handing out his phone number to her. It looked like things had taken a new twist in the last couple days.

Cary doubled up his fist and slammed it into the side of the phone. He yelped as pain shot up his arm. That was stupid, he thought, as he grasped his wrist and opened and closed his hand to be sure nothing was broken. That's all he would need—a busted hand before the dance Saturday night.

Then he thought about it. At least if he had a busted hand, he'd have a good excuse not to go. He opened his fist tentatively and wiggled his fingers. Nothing was broken. There was no such luck. Like it or not, he'd be playing at the dance on Saturday.

Yolanda came up the hall and saw Gigi leaning against the wall next to the phone, smiling. "What are you so happy about?"

"Things couldn't be working out better," Gigi said.

Jane looked at the messy page in front of her. It was her copy for the next week's editorial, and there were scratch-outs and arrows and inserts all over it. She just couldn't seem to concentrate. Nothing seemed to be coming together. Every time she had a thought and started to write it down, she would think about Beau, and that would start her thinking about Cary. Then she couldn't remember what she had been planning to say.

She finally slammed the notebook down on the bed next to her. This was stupid. She would just call Cary and explain things to him. He would probably understand. After all, it wasn't as if she had invited Beau to come see her. But now that he was here, she couldn't very well ignore him. This whole mess certainly wasn't her fault.

Jane untangled her legs and went out into the hall. She heard the laughter from Dee and Maggie's room. Toby and Andy were in there doing something for the party. She should be in there, too, she reminded herself. But she had that story to write first and she wasn't going to get anything done until she took care of things with Cary.

Jane went to the end of the hall and lifted the phone off the hook. She dialed his number with shaky fingers. What if he refused to talk to her or hung up on her? No, he wouldn't do that.

Someone answered the phone on the third ring. Jane asked for Cary. The guy said, "Just a minute," and dropped the phone on the other end, causing Jane's ear to ring.

After what seemed like a very long time, Cary came to the phone. "Yeah?" he said impatiently.

"Hi. It's me," Jane said.

"What happened? I thought you were too busy to call."

"Whatever gave you that idea?" Jane asked.

"Never mind. I just heard you were pretty preoccupied with all that entertaining you're doing over there. So, I just didn't expect to be hearing from you."

"That's what I wanted to talk to you about," Jane said. "I wanted to explain about Beau."

"Jane, if you called to tell me all about you and your new boyfriend, I'm not really interested."

"He's not my boyfriend. At least not like you think. I didn't invite him to come out here."

"No, I'm sure you didn't. It would have been a lot easier to keep him tucked away out in Texas and see him when it was convenient for you."

This wasn't going like she'd hoped. Everything was coming out all wrong. She wanted him to understand, but he wasn't even giving her a chance to explain. Beau had come a long way, and she had to be nice to him. It didn't mean that she and Cary couldn't still go together. All she wanted was for him to be patient for just one stupid little week.

"Cary, it's only for a week. After that, things can go back like they were."

"I don't think so, Jane. After all, you fell for some guy in a week. Maybe the same thing will happen to me. I got a chemistry test to study for. I'll see you around."

Jane stared at the dead receiver in her hand. She couldn't believe anyone could be so narrow-minded. Now what was she going to do? Well, who needed him anyway? If Cary wanted to call it off over something as silly as a visit from a friend, then she was better off without him.

She slammed the phone into the cradle. If she was so much better off, why did she feel like crying? Boy, this was great! She had called Cary to clear the air so she could finish her article, and now things were worse than ever.

By this time next week, her life would be over. Beau would be back in Texas. Cary wouldn't be speaking to her. And she'd get fired from the newspaper because she couldn't write that dumb article. The echo of laughter came out of Dee and Maggie's room and taunted her as she came up the hall. She was glad someone around there still had something to laugh about.

CHAPTER EIGHT

Toby and Andy sat Indian-style on the floor facing Dee and Maggie. The room smelled of pumpkins as the girls sat around the remains of the insides they had carved out. A discarded pile of stringy pumpkin innards and small oval seeds was on the newspapers in front of them. Everyone's sleeves were pushed up and their arms were sticky to the elbows.

The four girls were admiring Dee's latest creation. Andy sat it against the wall with the others they had already finished. She stepped back to admire them. They did look terrific.

There was a burst of laughter from behind her and Andy turned back around to see what everyone was laughing at. Toby had taken a carved-out piece of pumpkin and wedged it in her mouth like jagged teeth. It resembled the vampire teeth Andy and her brothers used to buy when they were little.

Toby was crouched over in a menacing position with her hands out like claws, moving around the room grabbing at the girls while she made growling noises. She looked too silly to be very scary, yet Maggie and Dee crowed with delight as she came toward them.

"Maybe you can go as the bride of Frankenstein," Dee said, falling against her bed in exhaustion.

Toby pulled the piece of pumpkin from her mouth. "I think I'll let Gigi have that one."

"Seriously, what are you guys going to wear?" Dee asked.

Toby sat on the bed. She tossed the discarded piece of pumpkin into the garbage can near the door. "I don't know yet. I kind of thought about making a hat from a baggie and going as the "Man from Glad." You remember him? He used to wear this white suit in all those dumb TV commercials and rescue ladies whose leftovers were dried up."

"That must have been a Texas commercial."

Toby swung the pillow at Maggie. "How about you?" she asked.

"I don't know."

Toby looked over at Andy, who was rearranging the pumpkins on the floor. "What are you going to be, Andy?"

"I'm not sure. I thought Little Red Riding Hood might be fun."

"I'm sure you could get some Oakley Prep guy to volunteer to be a wolf," Maggie said. The girls laughed.

"You know, Toby, with your red curls," Maggie said, "you'd make a great Orphan Annie."

"Or Raggedy Ann," Toby said.

"That's not a bad idea," Andy said with excitement. "You could be Raggedy Ann and Neal could be Raggedy Andy. It would be so cute."

"I'm not sure Neal would appreciate dressing up like some storybook character."

"He's a good sport," Andy said. "He'd do it. Ask Jane."

"I don't know," Toby said. Maybe Neal would dress up like Raggedy Andy, but would she want to be seen in public with him if he did?

The girls talked on about what each of them might wear to the dance. No one even noticed Jane come into the room. She had been so preoccupied with her own troubles, they had all been leaving her pretty much alone. Andy was still more than a little annoyed that Jane had done almost nothing to help get the decorations ready for the party. A definite coolness between them had developed.

Jane listened to their animated conversation from the doorway on how they might go about making the different costumes they had each dreamed up. After all, the party was in a few days, and they had to come up with something soon.

She hadn't even thought about costumes. The way she felt about having both Cary and Beau at the party, she would be happy to put a brown paper shopping bag over her head and go incognito. If neither of them recognized her, she wouldn't have to worry about what was going to happen.

Maggie looked over and saw Jane. "Hey, stranger. Did you come to check the progress we were making?" She got to her feet. "Look at these. What do you think?"

Jane followed Maggie over to the pumpkins against the wall. "They look great," she said with as much enthusiasm as she could muster. "I'm just sorry you guys are having to do all this without me. But I think I finally have that editorial finished, and I should have more time to help out now."

"That would be nice," Andy said. Jane looked over at her, and wished Andy would be more understanding. She certainly hadn't planned all this to happen the same week as the party.

"Did you see the sketches for the design we're going to use near the bandstand?" Dee held out a sheet of paper, which Jane took. There was a scarecrow made of sticks and straw standing among bails of hay with wooden slats resembling a fence behind him. Uncarved pumpkins sat around his feet.

"This is cute," Jane said, "but how are you going to build all this?"

"That's where Randy and Beau come in," Toby said. "We were hoping Randy would let us borrow some hay. And I'm sure that he and Beau will help us with the fence posts. I know both of them have built enough fence around their places to know what they're doing. Anyway, we think it'll look great when they get done."

"It will," Jane agreed. "I'll tell you what. Since I'm not really doing my share around here, why don't I talk to Beau and Randy about helping us build this Saturday morning. And I'll even take charge of seeing that it gets done while you guys handle the rest of the decorating."

"That would really help," Andy said. "We're going to be lucky to get everything ready by Saturday night."

"I'll go with you to Randy's place, Jane," Toby said. "With you working on Beau and me working on Randy, they won't be able to say no even if they wanted to."

Andy looked at the clock on Dee's desk. It was nearly nine-thirty. They had been working on the pumpkins since right after dinner. She still hadn't studied for her math test. "We'd better get back to the room," she said getting up from the bed. "At this rate we'll all be too tired to enjoy the party when we get there."

Everyone said good night and the three of them went back to their own room. Jane went to her desk and picked up her papers and waved them at Andy and Toby. "All finished," she said proudly.

"That your editorial?" Toby asked.

"It sure is."

"How is it?" Andy said.

"Well, it won't win any Pulitzer Prizes, but at least it's done."

"That's good. Now maybe you'll have time to help us. You know these next few days are going to be really hectic."

"Don't worry. I'm planning to devote all the time you need to helping you guys make this the best party ever."

While the girls were busy planning what to wear at Baker House, Gigi and Yolanda were doing a little planning of their own. They had pretty much decided how they would do the haunted house, using black plastic stretched across portable room dividers to make individual chambers.

"We want this to be the scariest thing since *Nightmare on Elm Street*," Gigi said.

"With the boys from Oakley Prep helping us, it should be really good," Yolanda agreed.

"Yeah, but we're not going to just count on that," Gigi said, "I have a few other things in mind to spice up the whole thing. Things guaranteed to make those girls scream so loud, you won't even be able to hear the band."

She sat on her bed, a smile breaking across her lips. "And if I'm lucky, the leader of the group will come in to see what's wrong, and the two of us will talk about it."

Yolanda got up on her knees and turned to face Gigi. "Won't Jane Barrett just die?"

"You bet she will. And there's not a thing she can do about it because she'll be stuck with that other guy, and she can't very well leave him standing there all alone while she tries to win Cary back.

"But the best part will be after the party when that guy goes back to Texas, and Cary is with me, and she's got nobody."

"Oh, Gigi, that would be *too* funny." Gigi looked into Yolanda's admiring face. Sometimes she was a pain, but she was always loyal, and no matter what scheme Gigi thought up, Yolanda went along with it. Gigi was pretty lucky to find someone like Yolanda in this school full of drips.

She wondered if her parents would have planted her here if they'd had any idea what kind of place it really was. But she thought they might have. They were too busy running all over the place to worry about whether or not she was happy.

Gigi imagined if it had been possible to send their maid to the school for the parent-teacher conferences instead of going themselves, her parents would have done it.

"Is something wrong, Gigi?" Yolanda's voice brought her back to the present.

"No, everything's going to be just perfect." She got off her bed and went into the hall. "I'll be back in a minute," she called over her shoulder to Yolanda.

She dialed Cary's number and planned her strategy. "Hello," a male voice said on the other end.

"Cary Slade, please," Gigi said.

"Just a minute. I'll see if he's in."

She tapped her foot and traced the edges of the phone with her long manicured nail while she waited for Cary to come to the phone.

She heard the rattle of someone picking up the phone. "This is Cary."

"Hi, Cary. It's Gigi. I wanted to know if you'd found anybody to help in the haunted house yet."

"Well, actually, I haven't really asked around much yet. I'm sorry."

"Oh, that's okay. I know how busy you are. That's why I'm calling. I thought I might come by the school tomorrow after classes and talk to some of the guys myself. Do you think you could meet me someplace and show me around?"

"Well, um. . . ." Cary tried to imagine himself walking around campus with Gigi Norton at his side. He could really think of a lot of things he'd rather be doing.

"I hate to ask you, but I don't really know anyone else." Gigi tried to make her voice sound as sweet and appealing as she could.

"Yeah, sure," he said with a shrug. "Look, I'll meet you at the student center about four o'clock. Will that give you enough time to get over here after your last class?"

"Oh, more than enough. I really appreciate this," Gigi said.

"No problem," Cary said. He hung up the phone and wondered what Jane would think if she saw him escorting Gigi Norton around. Well, who cares what she'd think? Why did *he* care? She was plenty busy herself these days. Maybe he'd like her to know that he was escorting Gigi around. It just might serve her right to give her a dose of her own medicine.

Gigi came back into her room. Yolanda was still sitting on Gigi's bed where Gigi had left her. Just like a faithful puppy, Gigi thought.

"I may not be here for dinner tomorrow," Gigi said as she draped herself across the chair near the desk.

"Where will you be?" Yolanda asked.

"I have an appointment at Oakley Prep." Gigi looked at Yolanda and a wicked smile broke across her face. "With Cary Slade."

"What is Jane going to say?"

"Jane isn't going to find out. At least, not yet. When I'm ready, I'll make sure she knows. But right now, I think it's better if she keeps very busy with that cowboy of hers."

CHAPTER NINE

Beau managed to keep himself busy at Randy's during the day while Jane was in class. Like most country people, the Crowells weren't much for sleeping in, which was okay with Beau, because he couldn't seem to get the hang of it, either. After so many years of getting up at dawn, his body just automatically quit sleeping.

He would go downstairs to the delicious smells of early morning breakfast cooking. Ms. Crowell would pour him a cup of her fresh-perked coffee, and he would sit at the table and watch her bustling around the kitchen. He had offered to help her numerous times, but she'd just throw her hands up and say, "Oh, land sakes, I've been doing this alone for twenty-seven years. I wouldn't know what to do with help if I had it."

Thursday morning, the house seemed

particularly chilly in the upstairs bedroom when Beau opened his eyes. He rolled over and read the clock. It was nearly six-thirty and still dark outside. He sat up, draping the warm patchwork quilt around his shoulders as he got out of bed and went to the window. He pulled the curtain back and watched the softly falling snow drift past the cold glass to the white ground below him. It seemed early for snow. He stood at the window and marveled at the beauty of the untouched white landscape.

Beau went back to the bed and tossed the quilt off. He picked up his jeans from the foot of the bed and pulled them on, shivering at the coldness of them. He could hardly wait to get downstairs. Already he could smell the coffee brewing and almost feel the hot cup in his hands.

Toby was also looking out at the early snowfall. It was beginning already. That oppressing winter weather that would settle in on them and last for months. She was glad she had the party to look forward to this weekend and Neal's upcoming visit.

She padded down the hall to take a shower and heard soft voices drift out of the various rooms. Toby stood beneath the warm spray and relished every moment of it, knowing the cold that awaited her when she went out that day.

Toby came back into the room to find Andy stirring, too. "Did you see the snow?" she whispered in animated excitement.

"Yeah," Toby said, a little less enthusiastically.

"I just love the first snowfall of the year." Andy went to the window to look at it. There wasn't much snow. Just enough to cover the ground with a blanket of white. She could still see the tips of the grass peeking their tops through in places as they, too, tried to hold off the onset of winter.

Jane stirred in her bed and opened one sleepy eye. "What are you two looking at?"

"Snow," Andy said.

"Really?" Jane got up and came to the window. It amazed Toby that these two girls who saw snow every winter of their lives could get so excited about it. Then she moved in behind Jane and Andy. It did look pretty. The three of them stood huddled closely together, feeling the warmth of each other as they watched the snow mark an official beginning to winter.

By afternoon, the sun had come out and much of the snow had already melted. Jane and Toby were going over to Randy's to talk to Beau and Randy about the decorations. Both of them watched the clock during their last class and listened very little to what was going on. When the clock's hands finally dragged themselves around to three o'clock, the girls fairly burst out of class.

Climbing the fence between Randy's and the school, the girls were laughing and making so much noise, that even from inside the house, Randy and Beau heard them and came out. "What's up?" Beau asked.

"We came visiting," Toby said.

"Yeah, we're here to talk you into helping us on Saturday," Jane added.

"I don't know about this," Randy said, looking over at Beau. "Help you do what?"

"We have this great idea," Jane said, pulling the sketch from her pocket, "and we need your help to build it." She handed it to Beau, who looked it over and gave it to Randy.

"That doesn't look too tough," Randy said with a shrug. "We'll just throw some hay and wood into the back of the truck and meet you at the school about nine Saturday morning."

"And bring some old clothes," Toby said. "We need to dress up the scarecrow."

"Why don't you come on in with me and pick out what you want?" Randy asked. The two of them started into the house. "You guys coming?"

"You go on," Beau said. "My days here are numbered. I think I'd like to take a walk instead."

He took Jane's hand, and they walked up the path that had been made by the many horses' hooves over the years. It was hard to believe it was already Thursday afternoon, and he would be leaving so soon. When Beau had gotten here, a week sounded like a long time, but as he reflected over it now, it didn't seem long enough.

Beau stole a sideways glance at the pretty girl at his side. Like it or not, he was falling in love with her. As unlikely as it seemed that he would pick someone so unsuited for ranch life, that is just what he had done. He wondered what his folks would say if he brought her home with all her Boston airs. Then he wondered what *her* folks would say if she brought him home with his Texas accent and his down-home ways. He smiled at the thought.

"What's so funny?" Jane asked.

"I was just trying to imaging myself sitting in your parlor drinking coffee out of little china cups and shooting the breeze with the old Barretts of Boston."

Jane laughed. "Well, to begin with, you would be in the sitting room, not the parlor, we serve tea, not coffee, and we make polite conversation. We don't 'shoot the breeze.' "

"Whatever you do, I can just imagine me doing it. Shoot, I'd look even more out of place than I do here."

Gigi Norton was also taking a walk. She strolled through the campus of Oakley Prep with Cary by her side and felt all the curious stares as they went by. She was sure that most of them knew Jane and were wondering why he was with someone else. Get used to it, she thought. If I have anything to do with it, this is the way it's going to be.

As they walked along, she studied his handsome face. His finely chiseled cheekbones and straight nose gave him almost a model's profile. He was very attractive. That Jane Barrett was even dumber than Gigi thought to let this one get away.

Cary felt her eyes on him and turned to look at her. He smiled self-consciously at her before looking away again. Gigi was staring so intently at Cary, she stepped off the sidewalk and twisted her ankle. She yelped as she grabbed onto Cary's arm.

Cary instinctively threw his arm around her and held her up. "What happened? Are you alright?"

Gigi turned her big brown eyes on him and said, "I twisted my ankle. I'm not sure I can walk." Actually, she realized almost immediately that she could walk just fine. But why pass up a great opportunity like this? She had her arm around his neck and he scooped her up.

"Here, let me get you to this bench over here." He carried her to the bench and sat her gently down. Then he knelt beside her and touched her ankle. The trace of his gentle fingertips sent a chill up her spine. She looked at the top of his head and watched the sun reflect off his soft, light brown hair. She couldn't resist a little smile at how well things were working out.

"Where does it hurt?" His fingers gently probed the indentations of her ankle. She let out a little yelp at the appropriate time, and he pulled his hand away as if he had touched something hot. "I'm sorry. Do you want me to take you to the infirmary?" He looked up at her with concern in his eyes.

"I think it'll be okay. Can we sit here a minute? I'm sure I'll be fine."

"Sure." Cary stood up and sat beside her. Actually, it wasn't as close as she would have liked, but that would come in time. He gave her the same adorable smile he'd flashed her just before she'd lost her balance and then he quickly looked away.

"I'm sorry about lousing up your whole afternoon this way," she said.

"Oh, you're not. I didn't have anything to do anyway."

"Maybe I can buy you a pizza in Greenleaf for all your trouble then."

"Are you sure you feel up to it? I mean, with your ankle and all." Cary was kicking himself. Why hadn't he told her he had a major paper to write or a biology exam? Something. Anything to keep her from thinking that he wanted to spend more time together.

Gigi lifted her leg and slowly rotated her ankle. "It feels much better. I think it was just one of those things where it stings for a minute and then it's fine."

"Well, if you're sure you're all right. . . ." He got up and Gigi did, too. She took hold of Cary's arm.

"If I just hold onto you, I'm sure I can make it easily." She limped along next to him, being careful not to limp too much so as to make him think she needed a doctor. After all, she only wanted to get his attention and sympathy. Not spend the evening in some infirmary waiting forever for X-rays that would show nothing.

Beau looked down into Jane's beautiful face. "Don't go back to the school tonight, Boston. Let me take you to Greenleaf for dinner."

"A pizza does sound inviting," Jane said. She wanted to spend as much time as she could with him. She was thinking of Beau's upcoming departure and knew she would miss him. Seeing him again had been wonderful. She thought, I could get used to coming to the ranch and finding him here.

Then she thought about what he had said earlier. What would her parents think if she were to bring him home? It probably wouldn't be any worse than the reaction they had had the first time they'd met Cary.

Thinking of Cary, she couldn't help but wonder how he was tonight. She would have to straighten things out between them after Beau went home. She looked at Beau and realized she liked them both. They were so different, and yet she liked them both so much. She was only sixteen. Why should she have to choose between them now? It was unfair.

It was almost dark when they got to Greenleaf. The lights of Pizza Pete's were as inviting as the tantalizing smell that wafted outside. They chose a table near the free-standing fireplace in the center of the pizza parlor. The warmth of the fire was not only inviting, but also romantic.

Beau asked what she wanted on the pizza and then went over to order for them while Jane went into the women's room to freshen up. She looked at her reflection in the mirror. The crisp air had given her rosy cheeks. She didn't need any makeup to add color tonight, that was for sure. Realizing she didn't even have a brush with her, Jane fluffed her full blonde hair with her hands. It wasn't great, but it would have to do. Besides, Beau had seen her looking much worse — like the day he'd stopped by Toby's and she had been cooking Andy's disastrous dinner. She'd had flour all over her face and her hair had been a mess.

She came out of the bathroom and saw Beau pouring Coke from a pitcher. He had taken off his vest and looked so at home sitting by the fire. He was wearing a navy and tan wool sweater that looked more Vermont than Texas. He was so good-looking, Jane couldn't help but stare.

She sat down across from him. "Coke all right?" he asked. "I forgot to ask you, and I just took a chance that you wouldn't mind. If you want something else, I'll order it."

"No, Coke is fine." She picked up her glass and took a sip just to prove it to him.

She set the glass back down on the table, and he reached across the table and took her hand. She looked into his deep green eyes and watched the reflection of the dancing fire set them aglow. She thought again of how much she would miss him.

The spell was broken when the door opened and a blast of cold air came across them. Jane looked up and nearly fell out of her chair. Gigi Norton was coming in, holding onto Cary's arm and smiling up at him. She quickly pulled her hand out from under Beau's and dropped it in her lap. All the warmth of the fire seemed to dissipate, and she felt a cold knot in the pit of her stomach.

Gigi Norton! Of all people. Why had he chosen to show up here with Gigi Norton? Beau looked over at the two people coming in the door. At the same time they looked over and saw him.

Gigi held tighter to Cary's arm. This was even greater than she had hoped for. It couldn't have worked out better if she'd planned it. Who would have believed it?

Cary's first instinct was to shrug Gigi's arm off him. Then he saw Jane sitting there with that guy, holding his hand, and instead he took his own hand and placed it over the top of Gigi's. He saw the look of shock on Jane's face, and he was glad. It served her right. Let her think what she wanted.

"Pizza for Beau," The loudspeaker said. Beau got up to get the pizza. "S'cuse me. I'll be right back." He went to the counter, leaving the three of them to stare at one another.

Cary was the first to break away. He took a firmer hold on Gigi and said, "Come on, let's order." Gigi flashed Jane a triumphant smile.

Beau set the pizza in front of them and Jane's stomach rolled over. "Wasn't that the guy you introduced me to the other day?" He pulled off a slice of pizza.

"Yes. And I'd rather not talk about it anymore if you don't mind." She took a piece of pizza from the other side and bit into it. It didn't seem to have any flavor as she chewed it up. She forced herself to swallow it and felt it roll down into her stomach and settle there like a rock.

Gigi and Cary sat on the other side of the crackling fire from them. Jane couldn't see them anymore but every once in a while she could hear their laughter. What could they possibly be laughing about? Just the other day, Cary had told her Gigi wasn't his type. Now there he sat with her.

Cary was also aware of Jane's presence on the other side of the fireplace. What was she thinking right now? Whatever it was, he hoped it was making her as miserable as he was. He looked at the girl sitting across from him and more than anything wished it was Jane. But she was with another guy.

She had looked so pretty when he walked in. He wasn't sure if her face was glowing from the warmth of the fire or the excitement of the guy she was with. Cary wanted to get up and walk out. He wasn't hungry anymore. He wondered if Jane was eating.

Jane watched Beau pull off another piece of pizza. She was still working on her first slice. If she could only recapture the same closeness they had had before Gigi and Cary walked in, it wouldn't matter who else was there.

Jane looked across the table at Beau's handsome face. A peal of laughter rose up and floated across the room. It was no use. All she felt was a desire to run away.

CHAPTER TEN

"Gigi Norton!" Jane howled. "Can you believe that? Gigi Norton."

"Maybe it wasn't what it looked like," Andy offered.

"She was holding his arm and he had ahold of her hand. What else could it be?" Jane sat down on her messy bed and crumpled into tears.

Toby and Andy came to either side of her. "He was probably just trying to get even with you for Beau," Toby comforted.

"How could he know we were going to be at Pizza Pete's? *We* didn't even know we were going there. It had to be a real date."

Andy looked across Jane's bent head to Toby. Could it have been a real date? It didn't seem likely. Even if Cary was mad at Jane, it was hard to imagine that he'd take his anger out on her by going out with someone like Gigi Norton. Still, they had met last Saturday and Jane had said that Gigi *was* flirting with Cary.

"Why would Cary be with her?" Jane said again. "If that's the kind of girl he wants, what does that say about me?"

"He probably doesn't know her." Andy said. "Look, he's feeling dejected right now and she comes into his life and makes him feel great, so he takes her for pizza. It's no big deal."

"To me it is." Jane rolled back onto her bed and buried her face in her pillow.

Andy and Toby got up and went to the other side of the room. "Maybe someone should warn him about her," Andy said. "Gigi's such a snake in the grass that I just know she's laid a trap for him."

"I think we should just stay out of it," Toby said. "Beau is leaving in a couple days. Cary and Jane can straighten things out after that. Let's go over to Dee's room and see how our pumpkins are holding up. Listen, Jane, we'll be right back, okay?"

When Jane heard the door close, she sat up. She had heard what they had said about warning Cary about Gigi. She owed him that much. Even if they never saw each other again, she couldn't let him get involved with a person as rotten as Gigi Norton.

Jane pushed herself off the bed and went down the hall. With trembling hands, she dialed Cary's number. After several rings someone answered the phone. "Is Cary Slade there?" Jane asked, barely recognizing her own voice.

When Todd came in to tell Cary he had a phone call from some girl, Cary groaned. "What are you complaining about? I'd give anything to be as popular as you've been around here this week. If you got a couple extra girls you don't want, send them my way."

Cary just might do that. He knew it was Gigi again. When he dropped her off after the pizza, she had waited expectantly for him to kiss her good night. He had feigned ignorance and patted her on the shoulder instead. Something flashed across her face. He wasn't sure if it had been anger or shock or what. Then she had smiled and reminded him that she would see him on Saturday night.

Cary watched her walk into Addison House and noticed she was hardly limping at all. It crossed his mind that the whole thing had been a put-on. But then he decided against it. It didn't make sense.

It had turned cold again, and Cary had driven his hands deep into his pockets and hunkered down inside his jacket for the walk back to the car. In spite of the cold, he had stopped long enough to look at the lights of Baker House. He looked up at the fourth floor and counted over three windows from the end. The lights had been on in Jane's room. Was she in there? So what if she was? He wasn't going to drop by and ask how she liked dinner. He had gotten into his car and driven back to Oakley Prep where he had been sitting in his room sulking ever since.

He forced himself to his feet and went down the hall to the phone. He lifted the receiver and tried to think of an excuse to get rid of Gigi quickly. But the voice on the other end wasn't Gigi's at all. When he heard Jane's soft voice saying hello he had nearly dropped the phone.

"Hi," Cary said. Then there was an awkward silence.

"Cary, I just wanted to tell you that I want you to be careful with Gigi Norton. She's a user and a lot of other things, and she'll hurt you if you give her a chance."

"And you haven't done that?" he asked coldly.

"Not on purpose. I never meant to hurt you."

"Forget it. I'll survive."

"Please, Cary, I don't want to argue," Jane said, feeling the tears building in the back of her throat and knowing her voice was quavering into the phone. But she had to do this. She had to do it for Cary. "Gigi Norton is the worst person I've ever known.

She's scheming and cruel and — "

"Then the two of you should have a lot in common."

"How can you say that?"

"Do you consider it honest to meet another guy and hide him from me? That is, until he shows up here and you have to tell me the truth. You know, I think if I hadn't walked up and caught the two of you together, you never would have told me, would you?"

"Cary, I didn't call to talk about Beau. I just wanted you to know about Gigi before you got too involved with her."

"I know all I need to know." The phone went dead in her hand.

Gigi sat on her pastel floral bedspread and balanced the bottle of red nail polish carefully between her feet. She blew on her nails and then held her left hand up for inspection. Satisfied, she switched the brush to her other hand and began to paint.

She hadn't really needed a manicure, but she wanted to look her best if Cary dropped by to see her unexpectedly. She had started out getting even with Jane, but she had discovered something today. She really liked Cary. He was very good-looking and sweet and considerate. She could be all those things, too. They would make the perfect couple. Only she knew better than to let him slip away. She looked at her long, tapered nails. Once she took Cary Slade by the hand, he would never get away.

Gigi sat her nail polish on the floor beside her bed and stretched out, lying against the headboard. She put her arms over her head and waved her hands in the air above her head to fan her nails.

Yolanda came back from her shower. She sat on the chair at Gigi's desk. "Do you think he'll ask you out again?" Gigi flashed her a knowing smile.

So what if she had sort of altered the facts a little and told Yolanda that Cary had taken *her* for pizza? That wasn't as important as the fact that they had gone, and they had seen Jane and that other guy there. She closed her eyes and relived the moment when they walked into the restaurant and saw Jane and Beau sitting there and Cary put his warm hand over the top of hers.

Who cared if he was only doing it to make Jane jealous? He had done it. And he would do it again. Only in the future, he would be holding her hand because he wanted to be with her. She would make him forget about that wimpy Jane Barrett.

True, he hadn't kissed her at the door, but that would come in time. She knew that once she kissed him, he would look forward to kissing her again. There was no doubt in her mind that she could make him happy.

And the best part about it was all the time she was making the two of them happy, she would be making Jane miserable. She would make Jane pay for every lousy thing she had ever said or done to her.

She wanted to hug that cowboy who had showed up here and loused everything up for Jane. He would probably never know just how much she appreciated him.

Beau was lying on one of the twin beds in Randy's room staring at the ceiling. Randy was sitting across from him on the other bed, leaning against the wall, his knees bent and his arms resting on his knees. He was playing with a piece of rope, tying and untying various knots.

"You know, she's just so hard to figure out," Beau said. "One minute she's warm and affectionate and the next it's like something clicked off, and she's cold and distant. She's a puzzle alright."

"I've got to admit," Randy said, "I never would have thought that you and Jane would attract each other."

"I guess I wouldn't, either. But if you'd seen her last summer in that white bathing suit, her hair flying all over the place and that wild look of terror in her eyes, you'd have fallen for her, too."

"It doesn't sound much like the Jane Barrett I know."

"She was different back there. Here, she's so uptight. The only time she really relaxes with me is when we're alone." Beau sat up. "That's it. It's me that's making her uptight."

"Beau, what are you talking about?"

"It was okay to be with me out in Texas where nobody knew her. But here, I don't fit in. We were in town the other day, and I told Jane I was fixing to get some ice cream and the lady behind the counter started laughing. She asked Jane if I was for real and Jane got all red in the face and nodded. I didn't pay much attention to it then, cause I'm used to Yankees being kind of rude — "

"Watch it," Randy said. "You're staying with a Yankee."

"I'm sorry, I didn't mean you. You and your family have been terrific. But other people I've met out here. They get impatient if you don't know where you're going, or if you don't know what you want when you get there. I'm not used to that. Back in Texas, we're a lot more laid back.

"And I guess when Jane was out there, she was a lot more laid back, too. That's why things aren't working out here. I just can't fit into her world. It was probably a good thing I figured that out before this went on much longer."

Beau got to his feet. "I'm going to go on

up to my room. I've got some packing to do."

"I thought you were leaving Sunday. What about the dance? We already told the girls we'd help decorate on Saturday."

"It's not a big job. You can do it without me. In fact," Beau stopped and cleared his throat, "I think you can all do without me here just fine."

Beau closed the door behind him and slowly climbed the stairs to his room. He knew, now, how those rodeo calves felt after they'd been tossed on the ground and tied up while the crowd cheered around them. He'd seen them jump to their feet and run from the ring feeling defeated and beaten and just wanting to get out of there and back to the safety of the pen.

A chill had set in in the old house. He shivered. It would be good to get back to Texas. He didn't belong here.

Jane came into the journalism room and Ms. Bailey, the journalism teacher, signaled for her to come into her office. Jane went to the back of the room.

"Jane, sit down." She indicated a chair next to her desk. She took something off her desk that looked vaguely familiar. Jane realized it was her editorial. "Have you read this?" she asked.

"Of course, I read it," Jane said, with a

hint of a smile. Was Ms. Bailey kidding? "I wrote it."

"Did you?"

The smile slid from Jane's face. "Yes."

"Well, I'd be hesitant to admit that if I were you. This is a sloppy piece of work, Jane. It's not at all what I'd expect from you. I had to look twice at the name because I couldn't believe it was yours. What's gotten into you, Jane? Is something wrong?"

Maybe it was the compassion in her voice, the understanding look she turned on Jane, or just the fact that she was an adult and might understand. Whatever it was, Jane felt a flood gate open and release a torrent of tears. She found herself telling Ms. Bailey about what an awful week it had been with Beau showing up unexpectedly and Cary being upset because she hadn't even told him there was a Beau. And worst of all, her roommates were angry with her because she wasn't helping out with the Halloween party and right now she could care less about that stupid party.

Ms. Bailey came around and sat on the corner of her desk. She still held Jane's paper in her hand. "It sounds as if a lot has happened this week, and I'm sorry. But that doesn't erase the obligations you have to people. Your roommates are upset because you committed to do something and they counted on you to do it. I am not pleased

with what you've done here because you
have an obligation to me and to your readers
as well.

"Jane, you have to realize what your limits
are and not go beyond them. When you
spread yourself too thin, you end up trying
to do too many things and as a result, none
of them get done well. Do you see what I'm
trying to say?"

Jane turned her tearful face on Ms. Bailey
and nodded. "Now, I think you'd better
take this back and rewrite it for the next
issue."

"But what about this issue?"

"I've already found replacement copy."
Jane came out of Ms. Bailey's office, her
editorial in her hand. Had it really been
that bad? She slipped it under her pile of
books and sat down.

She was surprised to see Randy waiting for
her when she came out of her last class.
"Jane, I have to talk to you." He took her
by the arm and steered her toward a deserted area. "Beau is leaving in the morning.
He'd be gone already, but there were no
available flights."

"Leaving?" Jane asked. "But I thought he
was staying for the party." She had mixed
feelings of relief and fear. If he left, she
could straighten everything out with Cary
Saturday night. On the other hand, why

was he leaving before he had planned to? Was something wrong?

"Wasn't he going to say anything to me before he left?"

"He was going to write you a letter, he said. Ever since he decided to go, he's been moping around the house like a pup with his spirit broken. I wish you'd go talk to him, Jane."

"I will," Jane said. "Let's go."

The two of them took off across campus together. As they got to the fence near the orchard, Jane's heart was beating faster, and her stomach was a battleground of butterflies all crashing into one another.

They went in the back door. Randy's mom was rolling out pie dough. "Hi there, stranger. You come to see Beau?" Jane nodded. "He's in the other room watching television."

Jane set her books on the phone table. She stood in the doorway of the living room and watched Beau. He sat in a chair with his back to her, and he didn't realize she was there. She came around to the side where she could get a better look at him. He still didn't seem to know she was in the room. He had his hands folded in front of him and his knuckles were resting against his chin. He looked deep in thought.

Someone won the grand prize on the game show and screamed. Beau didn't even react. "What'd she win?" Jane asked.

Beau's head snapped around and he looked at her. "What are you doing here? I thought you were working on dance decorations."

"Randy told me you're leaving in the morning."

"Yeah."

"I thought you were staying until Sunday."

"Changed my mind." Beau looked away from her and back to the TV.

"Is it . . . does it have something to do with me?"

"It has everything to do with you, Boston. I wouldn't be here at all if it wasn't for you."

"I'm sorry."

"Not your fault. You can't help it I'm foolish."

"Beau, you're not . . ." Jane dropped to her knees beside his chair and put her hands on his arm. He pulled away from her.

"What would you Yankees call it then? It was a fool thing for me to come traipsing out here thinking I could find that same girl I knew last summer."

"I *am* the same girl."

"No, you're not. You're someone else out here, Jane. But I'm not. I'm still the same. I'm just a kid from Texas."

"So is Toby, and she adjusts."

"But I don't want to adjust. I *want* to be

a kid from Texas with a funny accent and down-home ways. I guess what's making me sad is, I know you could never be happy with that."

"But why do we have to worry about that now?"

"Because if we kept on seeing each other, sooner or later, we'd have to worry about it. So I'm just saving us both a lot of trouble before it begins."

"Look, you're here now," Jane pleaded. "You came all this way. At least stay till Sunday like you planned."

"Like I said before, coming here was the wrong thing to do." Beau got to his feet and crossed to the window.

"Please, don't go," Jane said softly. She looked at his strong shoulders and more than anything, she wanted to go over and put her arms around them. But she sat frozen on the floor, waiting for his answer.

CHAPTER ELEVEN

The excitement in Room 407 was the only thing higher than the noise level. Dee and Maggie had come over to model their costumes for Saturday night. Dee was dressed like a punk rocker with her hair all sprayed to stand on end and an assortment of cast-off clothing that didn't seem to match. "I'm Madonna," she announced. "Do you think I look like her?"

With her glasses still sliding down her pert nose and her decidedly California girl looks, she didn't, but not to hurt her feelings, they agreed that there was sort of a resemblance.

Maggie was wearing a pink leotard and tights with a long pink tail pinned to the back. She had made ears out of cardboard and painted them a darker shade of pink and attached them to a headband. She had done a great job with her makeup, and

Toby had to admit Maggie was one of the cutest pink panthers she had ever seen.

Andy showed them her own costume. She had taken a large clear plastic bag and cut holes in the bottom for her legs. She was planning to fill the bag with small colorful balloons and go as a bag of jelly beans.

"What a great idea!" Maggie said. "It's so original, but I'm not sure what TV character you're supposed to be."

"I was worried about that, too, until I realized, I'm a TV commercial!" Andy laughed and so did everyone else.

"What about you?" Dee asked Toby. "Have you made up your mind yet as to what you're going to wear?"

"I don't know. I'll feel dumb no matter what I wear."

"I still think you should go as Raggedy Ann. We'll help you get a costume," Maggie offered.

"Sure, we will," Andy said. She pulled one of her miniskirts from a hanger. "How about this?"

"Are you kidding? On you that's a miniskirt. On me it would be indecent."

"Come on, we can find something." The three of them pulled things out of the closet and held them up for Toby's approval. She would wrinkle her nose and shake her head at each new thing they produced until the floor was littered with discarded clothes.

Finally Dee yelled, "I've got it!" She ran out of the room and came back a few minutes later with the perfect dress.

"Where did you get that?" Andy asked.

"It was one my sister used in *You're a Good Man, Charlie Brown* a few years ago. I thought it might come in handy some day so I brought it with me. I'd forgotten all about it till just a few minutes ago. How about it, Toby?"

Toby looked at the dress that Dee held out to her. It looked like something a first-grader would wear. Still, she didn't have anything else and everyone was trying so hard. "Well," she said hesitantly, "let me call Neal and see what he's wearing, and then I'll let you know for sure."

"Good idea," Dee said.

Toby stepped over the pile of clothes that Andy had started picking up and went out to the phones.

Neal's mother answered the phone and Toby worked up her nerve to ask if Neal was there. She always felt funny talking to his mother. It wasn't that his mother had done anything to her. In fact, Toby barely knew her. She had met her briefly at the Barrett Landing Party last year, but that was all. Still, the few times she had called Neal, she had hoped that he would answer the phone himself.

When Neal finally picked up the phone,

Toby was happy to hear his voice, and reminded again of how anxious she was to see him tomorrow. "Hi, Neal. I just called to be sure everything is still on for this weekend."

"Are you kidding? I wouldn't miss this for the world."

"I wanted to ask you about the costume. Have you thought of anything yet?"

"Actually, the few things I've thought of are pretty boring. How about you?"

"Well," she hesitated. "The girls thought that Raggedy Ann might be kind of good. They found this awful dress for me to wear, but — "

"Hey, that's a great idea. With your red curls, you'd make a really cute Raggedy Ann." Really cute, he'd said. No one had ever thought her to be really cute in anything before. In fact, in grade school she if she was really anything, it was usually "really tall." And in junior high, she was probably "really one of the boys." But here was good looking Neal telling her that she was "really cute."

"And I could dress as Raggedy Andy," he was saying.

"You could?" Toby asked with surprise.

"Sure. This is great! I'll throw something together, and I'll see you tomorrow. I should be there about four-thirty. I'm leaving school early and driving down. My parents want me to get there before dark. So how about having dinner with me?"

"Sure, anything to get away from Canby Hall food."

"Thanks a lot."

"Oh, I didn't mean it that way. I'd love to have dinner tomorrow." Toby felt herself blushing. Why did her brain refuse to function when she was with Neal?

She heard him laughing on the other end of the phone. "I know what you meant. I'll see you tomorrow."

Toby hung up the phone and ran back to the room. "Raggedy Ann and Andy are on for Saturday," she called coming around the corner in her stocking feet and sliding to a stop just inside the door.

She sensed the festive mood had dissipated in her absence. Dee and Maggie were just leaving, and Andy was quietly picking up the last of the clothes from the floor. Toby looked over and saw Jane sitting at her desk with her head resting in her hands.

Toby went across the room to her own bed and flopped down on her back. She was getting awfully tired of this. Ever since Beau had arrived last Saturday, Jane had been like a manic-depressive, happy one minute and crying the next. Toby was glad he would be leaving Sunday. She couldn't stand this on a regular basis.

"You want to talk about it, Jane?" Andy

asked gently as she came across the room to put a comforting arm across Jane's shoulders.

"What's there to talk about? My life is over. That's all."

"Well, if that's all," Toby said from her own bed. Andy shot her a disapproving look, and Toby got the message.

"Is it Beau?"

"It's Beau and Cary and school and Ms. Bailey and journalism and everything."

Andy sat on the end of Jane's bed and reached a hand across to pat Jane reassuringly on the arm. "It can't be all that bad."

"Oh, can't it?" Jane pulled her editorial from beneath the stack of papers on her desk. "This is probably the worst piece of journalism Ms. Bailey has ever read and it belongs to me."

"I could fix that," Toby said sitting up. Andy and Jane both looked over at Toby in surprise. "I could write something and give it to her. Then she'd know what really lousy journalism was all about."

"Toby, please," Andy said turning her attention back to Jane and the paper in her hand. Toby shrugged. She was just trying to help out.

"And to top it off, Beau is leaving in the morning and — "

"What? I thought he was leaving Sunday." Toby said.

"What about the party?" Andy said.

"I don't care about the party." Jane realized how that sounded after Toby and Andy had been working so hard, and quickly added, "I mean, I care, but right now it's not my main concern."

"Just what is your main concern, Jane?" Toby asked. "Why don't you enlighten us? Is it that Beau is leaving or that Cary was out with Gigi or that your journalism teacher doesn't think you're the next. . . ." Toby couldn't think of any major authors. "S. E. Hinton."

"Who?" Jane said.

"Oh, she writes great books. She wrote one called *Tex* about this kid who loved his horse and — "

"Never mind, Toby. I don't want to be S.E. Hinton. I don't want to be anybody. Right now, I don't even want to be me. The way I feel right now, I would have to cheer up before I could get depressed."

"Why is Beau leaving?" Andy asked.

"He says his coming here was all wrong. He thinks I'm a different person than I was last summer. And he says he doesn't belong here. I went to talk to him, and I asked him to stay, but he didn't say anything. Finally, I just left."

"Well, I may not know much about writing or how to handle problems with boyfriends, but if there's one thing I *do* know, it's how to talk to Beau Stockton. I've been doing it since we were in grade school. I'll be back later," Toby said as she grabbed her jacket from the foot of the bed and ran out the door.

Toby found Beau still sitting in the living room of the Crowells' house where Jane had left him. Only now Randy and his father were sitting in there with him. They were all watching *Magnum P.I.*

Randy was the first to see her. "Hey, Tobe," he said. "Come on in and sit down."

"Thanks, but I just wanted to talk to Beau for a minute."

"What about?" Beau asked. All his cockiness seemed to have disappeared. He didn't even look like the Beau Stockton she'd known and fought with since she was a kid.

"Can we go someplace?"

"Sure." Beau got up. "How about out back?"

They came through the warm kitchen and went out onto the back porch. The light from inside the house filtered out onto the steps. "I hear you're leaving in the morning?"

"Yep."

"How come?"

"I got my reasons."

"Come on, Beauregard, you're not making this very easy. I've got a roommate back there crying her eyes out, and I feel responsible because if it hadn't been for me, this wouldn't be happening right now."

"What'd you do? If I'd left it up to you, you never even would have introduced us."

"You're probably right. But you met each other anyway, and you liked each other. Whether the rest of us thought you would or not isn't important. The fact is, you did."

"Well, liking each other isn't enough. We're just too different. I know that now. My staying here wouldn't accomplish anything. Why drag it out? I came up here thinking I was in love and the sad thing about it is, I think I still am. But it can't go anywhere, you ought to know that, October. We're the same kind of people. Ranchers. And people like Jane Barrett of Boston wouldn't fit into my world any more than I'd fit into hers."

"No one's asking you to change. When I first came here, I knew I'd never fit in, but I'm learning to be comfortable being myself. And I like it here. I want to go back to Texas someday, but that doesn't mean that I can't like what I find out here. I wish you'd stay. Don't go home with a bad taste in your mouth."

For the first time since Toby had come over, Beau looked up at her with his usual sly grin, "She was really crying, huh?"

"Yep."

"Then I reckon I oughta stay. No southern gentleman would leave knowing he was breaking a girl's heart."

Toby almost flew across the grounds to Baker House. She burst into room 407. "He's staying, Jane."

Jane looked up from her desk as if to ask if she'd heard right. Toby nodded. Jane jumped to her feet and hugged Toby in an embrace that almost took her breath away, just as the phone rang.

Jane picked up the receiver. "Hello," she said.

"Hey, Boston."

"Beau, Toby just told me that you're staying until Sunday. I'm so glad."

"I'm kind of glad myself. Hey, do you think that band will know the Cotton-Eyed Joe?"

"Don't count on it," Jane said with a laugh. She remembered that barn dance after the rodeo last summer and his trying to teach her the Cotton-Eyed Joe, among other dances. Now it would be her turn. "You're up north now. You've got to learn to act like a Yankee."

"Well, I don't know about that. I think part of my problem has been that I been trying to be somebody different since I got here. I think it's time to be just plain ol' Beau again. But I will save you a slow dance if you promise not to step on my feet."

"With those boots of yours, who would notice?" Then Jane remembered it was a costume party. "You are planning to dress up, aren't you? You're supposed to come as your favorite TV or movie character."

"Look, Boston, I'm staying for the party, but I'm not dressing up for it. There's a limit as to how much pride a guy can swallow in one day, and I think I've had my fill today."

Jane smiled. "Okay, Beau, you win. No costume. I'm just glad you decided to stay," she said more seriously.

"I'm glad I'm staying, too. But it won't change anything, Boston. We're still who we are."

"I know. See you tomorrow after school." Jane hung up the phone. What difference did it make if they weren't suited for a permanent relationship? Neither were she and Cary. But she wasn't planning to get married for a lot of years. All she wanted to do right now was have fun, and thanks to Toby, she would be doing that now.

Jane looked at her roommates with a smile on her face.

"Now that's more like it," Andy said. "What are you thinking?"

"I'm just thinking how lucky I am to have the best roommates in the whole world."

CHAPTER TWELVE

Toby paced around the room nervously. She checked her reflection in the mirror for the tenth time. The tweed wool slacks and emerald green turtle neck sweater accented her red hair nicely. Then she glanced at the pile of discarded clothes lying all over her bed. Had she chosen the best thing?

She was so unused to this. Usually a pair of jeans was just great for her. But since she'd come to Canby Hall, she had finally gotten to where she would wear something else every once in a while if there was something special going on. It was almost four-thirty, which meant Neal should be there any minute. And that was pretty special.

The door opened and Andy came in. She whistled and Toby spun to face her. "You look terrific in that."

"I do?" They had gone shopping a few

weeks ago, and Jane and Andy had talked Toby into the outfit. She wasn't sure she would ever wear it, but now she was glad she had it. "I thought it'd be nice to wear something besides jeans tonight."

Andy nodded her approval and came over to the bed. She shifted through the things lying in piles in front of Toby. "Well, I definitely think you picked the best thing."

"You do?" Toby's face was radiant. She normally had so much confidence that it was almost funny to see her so concerned about something like what to wear. But Andy realized that Toby's experience with boys was limited, to say the least. Having a boy notice her as something other than a prospective teammate was something quite new and a bit frightening.

"Well, I'd better get this mess cleaned up before he gets here," Toby said. She grabbed a handful of clothes and went to the closet. Andy picked up the remains of what was on the bed and followed her.

"Where you guys going tonight?"

"I don't know. We'll probably just grab a pizza or something. You know, sometimes I think good old McDonald's would be nice. Just build it right on the corner of town. It could be a regular gold mine, you know?"

"I have a better idea. Build it on campus. Or right in the dining hall, and you *would* have a gold mine."

The girls howled with laughter. Though it wasn't all that funny, it was a good way for Toby to relieve some of the tension.

"Hey, what's going on in here?" Jane said. She pushed the door open further and bumped Andy, who was standing near the closet with her hands full.

"We were just discussing the financial advantages to owning a McDonald's franchise at Canby Hall."

"My, that is funny." Jane said without much humor. She sat her books on her desk.

"How did it go today?" Andy asked.

"Much better. I have a rough draft for next week's editorial and even in rough form, it's better than the one I turned in last week."

Toby finished hanging up the rest of her clothes and stepped from the closet. Jane saw her for the first time. She stood up and came over for a closer inspection. "Toby, you look darling!"

"Darling?" Toby asked suspiciously.

"Well, you look great."

"That's better. Do you think Neal will like it?" Toby came out into the room and did a hesitant turn.

"He'll love it. But heck, Tobe, he loved you in jeans."

"I guess that's true." Toby looked over at the clock radio near her bed. It was a quarter to five. She hoped nothing had happened to him.

"Stop worrying," Jane said. "Neal's always a little late." Jane looked at Andy. "So, what's the plan for tomorrow?"

"We get up early and go over to the student center."

Jane made a face. "Couldn't we sleep in and start at noon? There can't be that much to do."

"There's lots. All the decorations have to be hung, and we still have to get back here and get ready ourselves. By the way, what are you wearing?"

"I really haven't thought about it yet."

"The party's tomorrow night! When do you plan to start thinking about it?"

"Well, Beau says he absolutely won't wear a costume, and I'd feel dumb all dressed up if he isn't."

"Well, you are on the committee," Andy said firmly, "and you will wear a costume. We just have to figure out what it's going to be."

A knock at the door interrupted their conversation. "Hey, Toby, you got a guest in the lobby," someone said from the other side of the door.

"Thanks," Toby said, her heart beating so loudly she wasn't sure anyone could hear her over the noise.

"Have fun," Jane said.

"Yeah," Toby answered nervously.

Toby came into the lobby and Neal had his back to her. He was watching some girls on the lawn, laughing loudly, as they threw themselves into piles of fallen leaves.

Toby came up behind him. "Hi."

Neal spun around. "I didn't expect you so quickly. I" — he stopped and looked at her — "Wow, you look terrific! I like that outfit."

"Oh, thanks," Toby said as if it was nothing. He didn't have to know she'd spent hours trying to figure out what to wear.

"Well, what do you feel like eating?" Neal asked as he pushed to door open and waited for her to go through. "We could have dinner at the Greenleaf Inn if you'd like."

"Oh, I don't know. Pizza Pete's is more my style. They also have spaghetti and stuff like that if you don't like pizza."

"No, I like pizza. I just thought you might like a change."

Toby thought about it. The idea of a thick mouth-watering steak did have lots of appeal to her. What the heck? "I'd love to have dinner at the Greenleaf Inn," Toby said.

Neal took hold of her hand. "Good. My car is right over here."

Toby loved the way he said "caaah" and "hee-ah" and various other words. He had such a funny accent. Of course, it occurred to her that she had a bit of an accent herself, although she felt it had faded quite a bit in the last year that she'd been away from Texas.

The thick carpet of the Greenleaf Inn squished beneath Toby's feet. The hostess sat them at a table near the fireplace. The high-back chairs curled gently around Toby's shoulders, encasing her in the warmth and comfort of the old inn. She was glad Neal had wanted to come here. He was more the Greenleaf Inn type than the Pizza Pete's.

She looked across the table at his handsome features. The firelight cast dancing shadows on his face. He had soft brown eyes that looked back at her with such understanding. Staring at him sitting opposite from her and knowing they had come here together was almost more than she could believe. Boy, what would the kids back in Texas think of her now?

"What are you thinking?" Neal asked.

"Just how perfect you look sitting here in this room."

"Why? Because it's stuffy and formal?" A smile broke at the corners of his mouth revealing even, white teeth that any orthodontist would be happy to claim.

"No, because it's sophisticated and charming," Toby answered. It was so easy with

Neal. Even though he was far more worldly than she, he never made her feel awkward and self-conscious. It had been like that since the first time they'd met.

The waitress came over to ask what they wanted. Toby had been so busy gawking around and daydreaming, she hadn't even looked at the menu, yet. Ever the gentleman, Neal asked her to go first. Just once couldn't he be a jerk and jump in ahead of her and give her time to decide what she wanted?

"You go ahead," she said. "I'm still trying to decide." She quickly began scanning the menu while she listened to what Neal was ordering.

"I'll take the filet mignon, medium rare, baked potato, and the salad bar, please." He handed his menu to the waitress, and she was as charmed by him as everyone else always was.

"That sounds fine to me, too," Toby said. She hadn't had time to find filet mignon on the menu, but she knew it had to be good, didn't it?

"Fine, the salad bar is through there, just help yourselves." The waitress collected both menus and left them to find their way.

Neal got up and came around to Toby, who was trying to scoot her chair across the thick carpet. "Allow me," he said, pulling on the back and giving her room to slip out.

The salad bar looked like a meal in itself. There was a huge bowl of shredded lettuce and a wide array of good things to go on top of it. They began down the line piling tomatoes and cucumbers and bamboo shoots and sliced raw vegetables on top of the plate. Toby poured buttermilk dressing on top of hers and decided there was a definite resemblance to Mt. Everest in her creation.

She went to the end of the table and found croutons and sunflower seeds and various other crunchy goodies to sprinkle on top. Her mouth watered as she put the finishing touches on her salad.

"Can you eat all that?" Neal wondered. For the first time she glanced at Neal's salad plate which held a considerably more modest amount of salad. Feeling embarrassed, Toby wasn't sure whether to put some of it back or just take it to the table and only eat half of it. Neal probably wasn't used to girls who could out eat him. But Toby had always had a healthy appetite.

"I guess I got a little carried away."

"Don't apologize. I think it's wonderful. I get so sick of girls who put a few pieces of lettuce on their plate and sprinkle a dash of pepper over it and say they're watching their weight. It's nice to see someone enjoy eating."

He held her chair out while she sat down.

He went around and sat across from her. Toby watched everything he did. She didn't want to make any more dumb moves. If she had just let him go first at the salad bar, she wouldn't be sitting in front of a salad big enough to feed King Kong.

Toby had intended to leave some of her salad on her plate, she really had. But everything was so fresh and crispy that she just couldn't help herself. She ate every bite and enjoyed each mouthful. Who knew when she'd get a salad this tasty again? She'd better eat up and enjoy herself because it could be a long time between invitations to the Greenleaf Inn.

The steak was almost as good as those cooked over mesquite chips back home. It had been months since Toby had eaten a good steak, and she relished every bite. When she pushed her plate away and looked across the table at Neal, he was studying her with a satisfied smile on his face.

Toby felt self-conscious under his gaze. "Is something wrong?" she asked.

"I was just admiring you."

"Why? Because I can eat you under the table?" Toby kidded.

"No, because you're so honest. I like being with you. You're like a breath of fresh air."

"Yeah, well . . . speaking of fresh air. I could use some after that meal. Would you like to take a walk?" Toby wasn't good at handling compliments and attention from boys. She hadn't had much of it.

"Sure." He got up and slipped his cashmere scarf around his neck and put on his camel wool coat. He was so preppy that Toby wondered what Beau would think of him. Most of the boys back in Texas wouldn't be caught dead in a camel hair coat.

Toby slipped on her own navy suede jacket and wrapped a scarf around her neck. She pulled her gloves on as they were walking out. The chilly wind whipped at their faces and tossed their hair. Toby snuggled down into her coat. She felt Neal's arm encircle her and pull her closer to him. His warmth was welcome.

They walked along main street, such as it was, and looked at the few things displayed in the store windows. Neal was studying the set-up of cookware in the hardware store. "This town must be a wonderful place to save money," he commented. "I haven't seen anything yet I'd want to buy."

Toby laughed. This town was almost a city compared to Rio Verde where she was from. Why, that town consisted of nothing more than a general store, a grocery, and a combination gas and feed store. She thought again of how many worlds apart she and Neal were. She began to understand what Beau had been trying to tell her last night.

Then she forced Beau and Jane and all their troubles from her mind. After all, she wasn't planning to marry Neal or even take him home to meet her father. They were just good friends. The thought of taking Neal home to her father caused a smile to break across her face.

"What's so funny?" Neal asked.

"I was just thinking about home."

"What about it?"

"Just how different it is from here."

"I'd like to see it sometime. I'm sure since it's where you're from, I'd love it."

Toby thought about Jane's reactions to her Texas home last summer and tried to imagine Neal there in her place. What would he look like diving into the swimming hole and coming up with his perfect hair all dripping wet? How would he look on a horse riding out across the prairie? Sneaking a sideways glance at his near-perfect profile, Toby decided the idea of Neal in Texas was certainly an amusing one.

At the end of the street, Neal pulled her closer to him. He was just a little taller than she was, and she could almost look right into his deep brown eyes. His arms encircled her. "I like you, October Houston," he said.

"I like you, Cornelius Worthington," she

answered. His face bent forward, and his lips touched hers in a gentle kiss. A man walking by them cleared his throat loudly and they broke apart. Though their kiss had been brief, it had sent sparks through Toby and left her weak in the knees. She shivered.

"I guess I'd better get you back to the car," he said taking her by the hand. "You're still not used to this northern climate."

It didn't take long to get back to Canby Hall. At least not long enough. Toby didn't want this night to end. Neal pulled up to the curb near Baker House. But rather than get out of the car, he shut off the ignition and turned to her.

"Let's try that again, in more private surroundings," Neal said softly. He leaned into her and put his lips on hers again. Toby closed her eyes and felt the delicious sensations of her first real kiss. She put her arms around him.

He broke free and nestled his head into her shoulder. The feel of his warm breath tickled her neck. Toby never thought she could like a boy so much. He lifted his head and looked intently at her before he kissed her again. Toby was glad he did. She kissed him back.

CHAPTER THIRTEEN

Jane felt as if she had just closed her eyes when Andy shook her awake on Saturday morning. Jane rolled over and read the large numbers on her digital clock radio. It was 8:45. She rolled back to the wall and feigned unconsciousness.

"It won't work, Jane," Andy said. "You're getting up now." Jane felt her warm covers being tugged from her fragile grasp and suddenly, her body was assaulted by the frigid morning air. She yelped and sat up, ferociously grabbing the covers back from Andy. Then she lay back down.

"Look, Jane, we are going to the student center. If you don't get out of that bed and come with us, your sheets may very well be filled with salt when you get back into them tonight." Andy went to her side of the room to finish dressing.

Jane lifted the covers and exposed one

eye from under her comforter. "This is cruel and inhumane, you know."

"I know." Andy continued to tie her high tops.

"Saturdays are for sleeping in."

"Not this time." Andy stood up and bounced on her toes a couple times to assure a comfortable fit of her shoes. Then she went to her dresser and took a long scarf from the drawer, which she wound around her neck. She tossed the last end over her shoulder and turned to look at Jane accusingly.

"I'm getting up," Jane said. She let herself relish one last instant of the comfort and warmth of her bed before she slowly pushed the covers back, wincing.

Toby came in from the showers, her hair a mass of tight ringlets. She shook some droplets of water from her head, sending a spray on Jane, who was cautiously making her way across the room.

"Yeeaaack!" Jane howled to the sound of Andy's laughter.

"Sorry, Jane," Toby said. She took the towel from around her neck and began rubbing it vigorously through her hair. Jane made a wide circle behind Toby and went to the closet. She pulled a pink and mint sweat suit from the hanger. It looked like the warmest thing she had on this late fall morning.

* * *

When they got to the student center, they found Gigi and Yolanda already busy at work behind a large make-shift wall consisting of a wooden frame with black plastic stretched across it and stapled into place. A large hand-painted sign read NO TRESPASSING!

Toby looked at Andy and Jane. "Who'd want to?" The sound of their laughter brought Gigi out from inside the structure.

"If it isn't the three stooges," Gigi said. "Well, I must get back to work." She stepped back and dropped the plastic sheet in front of her.

Dee and Maggie came in carrying the carved pumpkins in each hand. Toby, Jane, and Andy set down the bags of decorations they had been carrying and went out to help them bring in the rest of the pumpkins.

"She might not have loaned you her car if she'd known what kind of decorations you'd planned to haul in it," Toby said, taking a sniff of the pumpkin-scented air inside the back seat of Meredith's car.

"I'll leave a window open a couple of inches. It'll air out by this afternoon," Dee assured her.

Toby was carrying in the last of the pumpkins when she saw Neal's car pull up to the curb. He opened his door and jumped out. He saw Toby struggling to hold onto the four pumpkins.

"Let me help this damsel in distress," Neal shouted as he hurried to her side. Just as he reached her, one of the pumpkins slipped from her arm and shattered on the cold concrete at her feet.

"Ohhh," she moaned, "Dee is going to kill me."

"Blame it on me," Neal said. He shut the door and took two of the pumpkins from her hands. She looked down and saw that he had been splattered by flying pumpkin debris.

"Look what I did to you." Toby said. "I'm sorry."

"Don't worry about it. The pants can be washed, but I'm afraid the pumpkin is beyond help."

Toby looked down at the orange blob that had once been a carved pumpkin. "Maybe she won't miss it," she said hopefully.

They went inside the student center to find Andy already busy with putting table-cloths on the long tables that bordered the dance floor. Jane came in from the kitchen area and saw Neal. She dropped her stack of tablecloths on a table and ran to throw her arms around him just as Gigi and Yolanda emerged from their plastic for-tress. "Would you look at that?" Yolanda said. "She's got another one! How does she do it?"

"Well, I know one guy who won't be in her clutches much longer. A certain musician won't be hard to lure away from her after tonight." Gigi watched Jane and the boy laughing and talking while Toby and Andy looked on with goofy grins. "I've seen enough," she said, and walked back into the haunted house with Yolanda right at her heels.

"How's everything back in Boston?" Jane asked. Jane and Neal had grown up practically neighbors and their families had known each other for ages.

Neal was the boy her parents had expected Jane to marry. And she had been perfectly content with that assumption until the unconventional Cary Slade entered her life. After Jane met Cary and broke things off with Neal, everyone had been in an uproar, but now her parents had actually grown quite fond of Cary. Jane suspected that Neal was happier now, too.

Seeing Neal brought back a flood of memories. Including the ones she had of her first encounters with Cary. She still had strong feelings for Cary. She couldn't deny that. But, there was something about Beau that she found irresistible, too.

Almost like magic, Beau and Randy stood in the doorway. "Hey, lady, I got a load of lumber and a bunch of hay here," Randy called. "Where do you want me to unload it?"

Toby's face lit up and she ran to Randy's side, followed by Neal. "Randy, you're just in time." Toby turned and saw Neal behind her. "Oh, here's Neal. And this is Beauregard Stockton. His parents own the ranch next to ours back in Rio Verde."

"Nice to see you again," Neal said, extending his hand to Randy. He did the same with Beau, who took his hand, but not before shooting a glance at Toby that clearly asked: Is this guy for real? After all, the only boy he'd *really* met since he'd come to Canby Hall was Randy. Of course, there had been the brief encounter with Cary, but neither of them had Neal's mannerisms.

"Well, we'll get that stuff unloaded from the back of the truck if you'll tell us where you want it," Randy said.

"Let me give you a hand," Toby said.

"Me, too," Neal offered. Beau looked at Neal. Toby read his face plainly. He was wondering if Neal could manage to lug a bale of hay. She felt her protective instincts bristle.

They got to the back of the truck and Beau jumped up on the bed and grabbed a couple fence posts. "Here you go, partner." He handed them down to Neal. Neal took them inside, and Toby stepped up to take the next load.

"He a friend of yours?" Beau asked. She saw the twinkle in his eye, as if he couldn't wait to get back to Texas and tell everyone that October Houston had finally found a boyfriend and a Yankee at that.

"Yes, if it's any of your business." She pulled the fence post from his hand and almost socked him with it as she swung it around. The only thing that saved him was his fast reactions.

"Whoa," he said putting his hands in front of his face. "Sorry I asked." But he wasn't sorry. Toby could tell by the look on his face that he was glad to have something else he could tease her about. Well, so what? He was just as crazy about Jane. She felt a little satisfaction in knowing that she had something to hold over his head, too.

Andy, Dee, and Maggie finished the table decorations and began hanging ghosts while Toby, Jane, and the boys worked on the scene near the bandstand.

The sound of hammering brought Gigi and Yolanda out to see what was happening. Toby and Andy were just standing their scarecrow on his feet when Gigi came over to where they were working.

"Oh, my, isn't he cute," she said. There was no missing the condescending tone in her voice. Both girls turned around.

"I'm glad you like him, Gigi," Jane said. "After the dance we thought we'd give him to you. Seeing as you have so much trouble attracting guys."

"Well, obviously that doesn't seem to be one of your problems, does it?" She looked at Neal, who was oblivious to her stare as he struggled to get his fence post to stand upright.

"Better watch her, cowboy," Gigi said to Beau. "I think you're about to be tossed aside for better pickings."

Before Beau could speak up, Jane had crossed the space between them and glared menacingly at her. "Why don't you just crawl back into your cave over there, or whatever that's supposed to be, and hide under a rock where you belong."

They had all stopped working by now. Randy stood clenching and unclenching his fists, ready to pull the two girls apart if they went for one another. The electric stares between the two of them sent off a heat that could be sensed by everyone in the room.

"I believe I'll go finish the *haunted house* so that I won't have to worry with it later on. After all, the band is going to be setting up soon, and I want to be available in case Cary needs me." Gigi turned her back on Jane, but not before she caught a glimpse of the look she had hoped to see. She chalked up a mark for her side on her mental scoreboard. Looking at her current tally, Gigi decided she was going to emerge the clear winner when the game was over.

Meredith Pembroke came in, her cheeks red from the brisk wind that had begun to blow outside. "This looks terrific." She came into the room and surveyed the decorations with satisfaction.

"We're not done, yet," Andy said. "We're going to string angel hair along the hallway coming in so that it looks like cobwebs and drop spiders from the ceiling."

"Do you need anything in town?" Meredith asked. "I need to run into Greenleaf for a little while."

"I think we're pretty well set," Andy said.

Gigi emerged from the haunted house. "Ms. Pembroke," she called. "Why don't you come over and take a tour of the haunted house?"

"I'd love to." She looked at the other kids. "Have you all seen it yet?"

"Well, it's not officially ready for public display, yet," Gigi said. "We thought we'd give you a personal tour before tonight, though."

"I see."

"Go ahead," Toby said. "We have a lot to do so we can go home and get ready."

Meredith disappeared behind the plastic

sheet and the others all wondered what she would find in there. They heard noise in the doorway behind them. Everyone turned to see Cary and the rest of the band bringing in their equipment to set up.

"Hey, Andy, where do you want this stuff?" Cary called.

"Right up here." Andy went to the front of the room where they had set up the portable stage. Cary stopped and admired the scene they had built to cover the front of it.

"This is really shaping up." As he looked around, Andy noticed his gaze stop on Jane and linger there. Andy also saw that he saw Beau coming from the kitchen carrying punch bowls to the serving table.

Cary turned back to the stage and began telling the guys where to unload everything. Jane stopped at the sound of his voice. She watched him, looking so at home on the stage, as he supervised the setting-up.

Gigi and Meredith came out of the haunted house, and Gigi went over to Cary. "How's everything going?" she asked.

"We'll be ready by tonight. How about you?"

"Us, too. You are going to come see it, aren't you?" Gigi asked.

"Sure."

"I'll even to take you on a private tour." Gigi smiled at him, but Cary's gaze went over her head to Jane. He saw that she was watching them.

He looked back at Gigi and smiled broadly as he squeezed her arm with his hand. "I'd like that."

When Cary reached out and touched Gigi's arm, Jane couldn't watch anymore. She turned around and almost ran into the kitchen, colliding with Toby, and knocked plastic glasses all over the floor.

"Hey, what's going on here?"

"How could he?"

"Who? Beau?"

"Cary! How can he stand to talk to that girl, let alone touch her? Doesn't he know what a snake she is?"

Toby had no clue as to what Jane was raving about, but Jane didn't seem to care. "I mean, if that's the way he wants to be about it, that's just fine. I'm looking forward to a wonderful evening with Beau."

"I'm glad to hear that, Boston." Jane spun around and saw Beau coming into the kitchen. He put his arms on her shoulders. "Since this is my last night here, what do you say we make it one to remember?"

"You bet we will," Jane said. She was hoping they wouldn't be the only ones remembering. If she had anything to do with it, Cary would be doing a little re-membering himself before the night was over.

CHAPTER FOURTEEN

The three girls in 407 were dashing around the room without much conversation as they tried to pull together their individual costumes. Toby kept looking at her reflection in the mirror and wondering if she was really doing this to herself or having a very vivid hallucination.

Andy came up behind Toby and tied her apron at the back. She evaluated Toby with a critical eye. "I know what's missing," she cried. She took Toby by the arm and pushed her toward the chair at her desk. "Here. Sit down."

Andy pulled out a drawer to reveal a mixture of makeup. Toby shook her head. "Uh-uh. You aren't putting the goop all over my face."

"Just sit there and be quiet. It's only for one night." Andy leaned down level with Toby and went to work. She drew two small circles about two inches in diameter on each cheek with creme rouge. Next, she took a black pencil from the drawer and drew long eyelashes below each eye. Taking a lipstick pencil, she traced a heart-shaped set of lips slightly larger than Toby's own. She stepped back and admired her work. "There! Go have a look."

Toby went over to the mirror and looked at herself. With the makeup, she did look more like Raggedy Ann and less like an overgrown kid in a goofy dress. "I guess it'll be okay, just for tonight."

"Okay?" Jane said coming in from behind Toby. "I think you look terrific. You might even get the prize for best costume."

"Don't count on it." Toby noticed Jane's reflection in the mirror behind her. She was wearing army greens. "What are you supposed to be?"

"That is *who* not *what*, and I'm Major Houlihan from *M.A.S.H.*"

Andy came over to Jane. "Yeah. You even look kind of like her with the blonde hair and everything."

"That's the whole idea, isn't it?" Jane went over to her drawer and pulled out a pair of socks. "I had a terrible time trying to figure out what to wear. It finally came down to this or Wonder Woman, but I refuse to bare that much of my body for the whole world to see."

"But you've got a great bod," Andy said, stepping into her own costume.

"I'm not anywhere near in as good a shape as you, and you're hiding underneath a bunch of balloons."

"Help me with this, will you?" Andy asked.

Jane and Toby went to Andy's aid, filling the opening at her neck with assorted colors of small balloons. Jane tied the ribbon that Andy had laced through the plastic at the neck of Andy's costume.

Andy stepped to the center with her arms extended on either side and did a careful turn. "Well? What do you think?"

"I think you look like a beach ball with legs," Toby said. Jane's sharp poke in the ribs told her that probably wasn't the thing to say.

Andy faced them again. "Really?"

"She was only kidding. You look great."

Obvious relief flooded Andy's face. "Oh, good. Well, I'm going to go ahead to make sure that everything is ready."

"If you wait a couple minutes, Neal and I can give you a ride."

"I'd better walk. I don't think I could sit down in this anyway."

"What about tonight?" Jane asked. "Aren't you going to get awfully tired of standing up?"

"Who's going to be standing? I plan to

dance the night away." Andy tossed them a quick wave good-bye on her way out the door.

Toby looked at Jane and saw she was deep in thought. "Hey, you look pretty unexcited for someone who is on her way to a party."

"I just can't understand why things feel so different with Beau here. Last summer he was so . . . exciting! He was always funny and confident, and now he seems like someone I hardly know."

"You *do* hardly know him, Jane. But even so, you're right. He is different here. But this isn't his home. He's transplanted into a world that he doesn't know anything about and, believe me, it takes a while to adjust."

Even though Beau hadn't been one of Toby's favorite people when she'd lived at home, she was getting to know a different side of him and beginning to see the reason the two of them couldn't seem to get along: They were too much alike.

"I suppose so," Jane said. "There are times when he's his old self, and I really like him, and then there are times when I look at him and wonder what I'm even doing with him. I know every day we spend together is pulling Cary and me further apart, and I'm just not sure it's been worth it."

"Maybe that's something you'd better

think about next time you start flirting with some guy. Not everybody realizes you don't mean it, and those people who take you seriously can get hurt pretty bad." Toby picked up her coat from the foot of her bed. "I have to go. Neal's probably waiting in the lobby."

Toby's words echoed in Jane's mind after she'd left. Had she led Beau on, knowing all the time that she was only amusing herself until she got home? No, she didn't believe she had. He was the one who kept showing up everywhere they went. There had been nothing but sparks and fur flying for the first week after they'd met.

But then, she had found herself drawn to Beau and thoughts of Cary never even crossed her mind. They'd had fun at the rodeo and the dance, and she did say she would miss him. Why was Beau such an enigma? One minute she was drawn to him and the other she was wishing he'd disappear. Well, it wouldn't matter much after tonight. He was leaving in the morning. She might never see him again. And why did that bother her?

"Jane, there's a guy pacing around the lobby looking awfully impatient, and he's waiting for you," one of the girls from down the hall said as she passed by the door.

"Thanks," Jane called. She picked up her

coat and stopped in the mirror to adjust her green fatigue hat.

Beau was watching the stairs for Jane. When he saw her, his face broke into a smile. "Who are you supposed to be? General Patton? I figured you'd come as Betsy Ross or one of your other relatives."

"Well, at least I dressed up," Jane said.

"Hey, I dressed up. This is my best shirt." Beau grinned at her and took hold of her arm.

They got there early. There were only a few other people there, and it was mostly the decorating committee and the boys from Oakley Prep who were going to help with the haunted house. Jane saw that the band was warming up already.

"Hey, Jane," Andy called. "I got us a table right over there near the dance floor." Jane smiled and nodded. It figured. Andy would be on the dance floor all night anyway. She loved dancing. It didn't matter if it was ballet or rock and roll.

Gigi floated over to them dressed in a long pink evening gown with a cape of chiffon flowing behind her. She was wearing a tiara of rhinestones on her head. She looked at Jane's costume and tried to hide her smile. "I see you've come ready for combat."

"I'm supposed to be Major Houlihan from *M.A.S.H.*"

"Oh, Hot Lips."

"Right," Jane said dryly. "And what are you supposed to be?"

"A fairy princess." Gigi adjusted her crown with the tips of her long red nails.

"Well, it looks like we're both changing our image for a night." Jane grabbed Beau's arm and almost dragged him to the table Andy had saved for them.

As the people began filing in, the lights came down, and the band started to play. Jane and Neal were engrossed in a conversation about someone they knew from home. Jane was having a good time catching up on the latest gossip. Toby looked around the dance floor and watched the band.

But Toby wasn't the only one watching the band. Beau was aware that Jane's eyes kept drifting up to the bandstand. Beau looked over at Cary. What could she possibly see in that guy? He needed a haircut, and he didn't look like he'd done a hard day's work in his life. Was that the kind of guy Jane really wanted? Well, what did that matter? She was with *him* tonight and that was what counted.

Andy was the only one not watching, but doing. She had been on her feet all night. But that was no surprise. Everyone loved Andy. She was not only the best dancer at Canby Hall, she was also bubbly and fun to be with. Though she hadn't come with a date since Matt was out of town, she didn't lack for dancing partners. Even average dancers looked good with her.

"Well, are we going to sit here listening all night or are we going to dance?" Jane asked.

"I don't do that kind of dancing," Beau said.

"Sure you do. Just get up there and jump around. You'll look like everyone else." Jane grabbed Beau's hand and pulled him onto the floor before he could protest any further.

"What a great costume," a girl from Jane's English class said to Beau. "I bet you're supposed to be John Wayne, aren't you?"

"No, I'm supposed to be Beau Stockton."

"I never heard of him," she said and danced off.

A girl who was on the journalism staff with Jane pulled her date over to dance beside Jane and Beau. "I love your costume," she said to Beau. "You look just like a real cowboy. Wait! Let me guess, you're James Dean in the movie *Giant*, right?"

"That's it!" Jane said before Beau could say anything. "That's exactly who he is." The girl danced away feeling satisfied. "See how easy that was? Just agree with them." Before they finished dancing the next two songs, at least ten other people danced by and commented on Beau's "costume."

As the second song ended, Beau started to leave the dance floor. "I've had enough of this."

The band then began playing a slow song and Jane grabbed his hand. "Not so fast," she said. "This is the one I've been waiting for." Beau stopped and pulled Jane into his arms. As Jane closed her eyes and moved to the rhythm of the music, she was taken back to the first time they slow-danced together. Jane was aware of what had drawn her to Beau in the first place. She felt the strength of his protective arms. Why couldn't she just keep her eyes closed and glide through eternity like this?

On the fringes of the dance floor, Neal had coaxed Toby to try dancing. At first, she felt self-conscious about it, then she realized as she looked around, that no one else was paying any attention to them. She relaxed and was surprised at how easily she moved. Then the band began the slow song and Neal took her in his arms. She quickly picked up the rhythm of Neal's graceful movements. She closed her eyes and let herself float across the floor in his arms. She was afraid if she opened her eyes and saw herself dancing around the room with a guy dressed like Raggedy Andy she would start laughing, and that would definitely spoil the mood.

From the stage, Cary watched as Beau glided Jane around the room in his arms. He wanted to change the song right in the middle, but the rest of the band would wonder what he was doing. So instead, he picked up the beat. Jason, the bass player, leaned over and said, "Slow down, man, you're rushing it."

But even if he played the song at double time, it wouldn't be over fast enough. Finally, Cary sang the last verse. He set his guitar down and said, "That's it, guys. Let's take a break."

Almost before he got off the stage, Gigi Norton was there taking him by the arm. "I promised you a private tour of the haunted house, remember?"

Cary's first instinct was to pull away and go after Jane. But when he finally located Jane, she was making her way back to the table where she and Beau were sitting. He grabbed Gigi's hand and said, "I'm ready."

Before they could get away, Meredith Pembroke came up to the microphone and tapped it a few times. "Excuse me," she called to Cary. "Is this thing on?"

Cary jumped back up on the stage. "No. I'll get it for you." He felt for the familiar button on the underside of the mike and flipped it up. "There you go." He jumped back off the stage where Gigi was waiting for him. He managed to keep some distance between them even though she kept inching closer to him.

"If I could have your attention, please," Merry said. The noisy room began quieting down in stages. "Could I have your attention?" she asked again. "A group of us from the faculty have been busy judging your costumes tonight, and we've come up with some winners we'd like to announce at this time."

The kids moved back onto the dance floor and stood crowded around the stage. "First of all, for the most unique costume, the prize has to go to Andrea Cord. We've had suggestions as to what she might be, and we've finally come to the conclusion she must be a cold capsule." Everyone laughed as Andy came up onto the stage to receive her prize. "Tell us, Andy, what are you supposed to be?"

"A bag of jelly beans." The crowd laughed again.

"In the next category, we have the most authentic costume, and we've chosen the young man dressed as a cowboy who is here with Jane Barrett tonight." While the crowd applauded, Jane was pushing Beau toward the stage.

"I'm not going up there," he whispered furiously. "I'm not even wearing a costume!"

"You are now. Go up there and accept

the award, and please, agree to whatever she says. For me," Jane gave him a pleading look.

Reluctantly, Beau went up on the stage and took the envelope Meredith extended to him. "Would you like to tell us your name."

"Beau Stockton."

"And, Beau, who is it you are supposed to be tonight?"

Jane held her breath and squeezed Toby's hand. "A good old Texas boy."

"I'll kill him," Jane said when everyone started laughing.

"Jim Bowie."

Jane's grip relaxed and she wanted to hug Beau. She didn't know for sure who Jim Bowie was, but Meredith Pembroke seemed to know him and the answer satisfied her.

Cary was doing a little hand-clenching of his own as he stood at the foot of the stage and looked at the guy who had taken Jane away from him. He heard some girl near him whisper, "He's so cute," and he'd had enough.

Cary turned to Gigi and grabbed her hand. "Let's get out of here, huh?" Gigi eagerly lead Cary toward the entrance of the haunted house while everyone else continued to listen to the winners of various costume divisions.

Cary and Gigi stepped into the darkened enclosure and Cary felt the pressure on his hand grow stronger as Gigi tightened her grip. Gigi had signaled to Yolanda, who had stepped in front of the entrance to keep everyone else out if the awards finished before they had completed their tour.

"Hey, where are all those guys I rounded up for you?" Cary asked as Gigi lead him through the maze of plastic that was now deserted. "Looks like they ran out on you."

"That's okay. I don't mind if it's just you and me in here." Gigi stopped at the foot of a black coffin and leaned against the satin liner. Standing there in the eerie blue light, her face heavily made up, she almost looked like she belonged there. The idea nearly made Cary laugh, and he was taken by surprise when her arms quickly came up and drew his face to hers.

Cary was aware of the taste of her lipstick as she pressed her mouth on his before he pulled back.

"We'd better be getting back," he said. "Sounds like the awards are over and the band is probably wondering where I am." He took his handkerchief out of his pocket and quickly rubbed it across his mouth.

Gigi grabbed his hand just before he got to the safety of the exit. "Will I see you after the dance?"

"I don't know. I have to help load up all

the equipment and everything. I'll be pretty busy."

"I'm in no hurry," Gigi said. She leaned back against one of the support pillars and kissed the tip of her finger and held it toward him in a gesture of good-bye. Cary nodded quickly and pushed his way out. He gulped a mouthful of the fresh air. He felt as if he'd been suffocating inside the large plastic enclosure, even though there was plenty of room.

Jane was just coming back from the bathroom. She stopped when she saw Cary near the haunted house exit. "The band sounds great tonight," she said.

"Thanks. I saw you were enjoying yourself out there."

Gigi opened the back flap of the haunted house and saw Cary and Jane talking. She stepped up protectively beside him. "I was just giving Cary a tour of the haunted house."

"I see," Jane said coldly, looking at Cary. "I'm glad to know I'm not the only one enjoying myself tonight." She started back toward her table then she stopped and walked back to Cary and took the handkerchief from his pocket. She touched it to his lips. "You missed a spot." She dropped his handkerchief at his feet and walked away.

The band started playing again, but Jane didn't feel much like dancing. Andy watched from the dance floor as several people began taking the Kleenex off and eating the Tootsie Pops inside the ghosts that hung all around the room. She was glad they were enjoying them.

Andy finally made her way back to the table and fell into a chair as best she could, stuffed with balloons. "If they would just eat the pumpkins, too, we wouldn't have much to clean up tomorrow." She looked over at Jane, who looked as if she'd just lost her best friend. "Hey, why are you looking so down? This is a party, girl. Come on, let's have some fun!"

"I don't feel like dancing."

"Okay, then let's tour the haunted house."

Jane's face became expressionless. "Yeah, let's do that."

The two of them got up and started across the room. "Hey, wait for me," Toby called.

The three girls entered the dark entrance and were grabbed by hands covered in fake blood. Andy shrieked and a wicked laugh rose up from the darkness that could only belong to Gigi.

"Glad to see you could join us," the voice said. "Proceed straight ahead."

Several gory scenes awaited them in various cubicles. One held a man with a cardboard ax that looked very real. With a glazed look in his eyes he reached out for them. Jane and Toby moved on quickly, but he caught the back of Andy's plastic bag and dragged her toward him. By the time she broke free, she had several popped balloons and couldn't locate Jane and Toby.

She came into the last partitioned-off area where Yolanda was waiting with a blindfold. Andy's instinct was to refuse to participate in this part, but she couldn't let Gigi have that satisfaction. Being a good sport, she let Yolanda tie the blindfold in place.

"Welcome to Dr. Frankenstein's laboratory," Yolanda said in a voice that she hoped sounded like Peter Lorre. "What you are about to feel are the brains used to create the monster Dr. Frankenstein built." Yolanda placed Andy's fingers onto a cold slimy substance which was actually spaghetti.

"The next thing you will feel are the eyeballs." The power of suggestion was great. Andy could almost believe she was touching eye balls instead of green olives.

"And these are the live rats, the monster will feed on," Andy reached into a cage and felt something warm and furry. What she didn't realize was the rats she was petting were the ones Gigi had sneaked out of the science lab.

Gigi was planning to return them first thing on Monday morning before anyone knew they were missing. She had asked Mr. Alexander for the rats and he had said,

"Absolutely not." So Gigi had just borrowed them for the night. They were so tame and used to being petted, that they wouldn't bite anybody, but they'd scare them just the same. However, when Andy's blindfold slipped down and she saw her hand touching live rats she didn't stop to wonder where they came from.

She screamed in genuine horror and pulled her hand out so quickly that the cage came crashing down to the floor, releasing the three rats inside. They scurried out. Several people saw them rush by and a panic somewhat similar to a cattle stampede began. In the rush to get out of the haunted house people began knocking over the divider walls and plowing through the plastic. The fragile structure crumbled like a house of cards while all the while, Gigi and Yolanda yelled for everyone to stop.

Within seconds, the haunted house was a jumble of plastic on the floor. In all the commotion, the band had stopped playing, and people were milling around on the dance floor in a state of confusion. Meredith Pembroke was in a panic herself. Ms. Allardyce rushed across the floor to see what the trouble was and nearly stepped on one of the fleeing rats.

Thanks to the quick reflexes of some of the students, the rats were recaptured by the time the others had lifted the plastic to find out if there were any injuries. No one seemed hurt, but several people were holding onto their sides because the laughter was bringing tears to their eyes.

Gigi crawled out from under the plastic sheeting with her hair, which had been piled on her head, sitting lopsided like the Tower of Pisa and her tiara hanging down over one ear. Jane and Toby, who had been comforting a frightened Andy, broke up at the sight of her.

"Andy Cord, you've ruined everything!" Gigi shouted above din of noise around her. "I'll get even with you if it's the last thing I ever do."

"If anything, I'd say you owe her a vote of thanks. You were the one who wanted everyone talking about your haunted house for years to come," Toby said. "Now, thanks to Andy, it looks like they all will be."

Gigi stood in the center of the ring of students. Everywhere she looked, she saw people laughing at her. Then her eyes met Patrice Allardyce's. Not everyone was laughing.

CHAPTER FIFTEEN

The early sun filtered through the long windows of the student center and illuminated the scattered remains of last night's party. Jane, Andy, Toby, Dee, and Maggie stood in the doorway and wondered where to begin. Dee looked over in the corner where the haunted house had once stood. "At least we don't have to clean that mess up." The five girls laughed.

"Okay," Maggie said, "Dee and I will take the tables. Andy, you can get the rest of the ghosts off the ceiling, and Jane and Toby can start taking down the scarecrow."

"Sounds good to me," Toby said. She and Jane went to the stage area and started breaking down the fence.

"Would you like a hand there, little lady?" Jane looked up. Beau was standing at her side, holding a hammer, his boot propped on the edge of the stage.

Jane straightened up. "Thanks," she said. He stepped in and quickly dismantled the fence.

"Why don't we get this stuff out to Randy's truck so we can load it up and take it out of here for you," he said picking up a bale of hay.

Jane picked up two of the fence posts and followed him out. In the back of the truck, Beau folded his arms, leaned against the cab, and looked at Jane. "What are you doing?" she asked. She put her hand self-consciously to her hair, thinking she must be a mess.

"Just trying to memorize how you look before I go."

"What time does your plane leave?" Jane asked.

"I've got time." He jumped down from the truck. "Come on, Boston, let's take a walk." Instead of putting his arm around her or reaching for her hand, Beau put his hands in his pockets as they walked.

"I guess coming here unannounced was kind of a rotten thing to do to you. But I was sort of afraid if I called first, you'd tell me not to come. I know I caused you a lot of trouble, but I'm not sorry I made the trip."

He stopped and faced her. "I like you, Boston, I really do. But I figure once I get back to Texas, it'd be the best thing for me to date around some, and I know you're going to want to keep seeing that musician, though I can't figure out why."

Jane started to protest, and he held up his hand to silence her. "I'm not saying that nothing will ever come of us, but heck, what's a good relationship if it can't stand a little testing?"

"You're right," Jane agreed. She looked into his trusting eyes and felt more for him than she ever had before.

"Sometimes you can keep your grip on something a lot better if you open your hand a little." He put his arm around her shoulders and pulled her to him. "I hope you'll come out to Toby's again next summer, Boston. You got a lot to learn about me before we make any plans."

Jane stepped back and looked at him. "I think you have a little learning to do yourself, Mr. Stockton."

"Maybe so, but we got plenty of time to do it. We're neither one in a hurry." He gently kissed her. The sound of Randy honking the horn broke their embrace. "I'd better get going, or I'll miss my plane."

"I'll write," Jane called to him.

"Well, there's something you should know. . . ."

"You can't read?"

"No," he laughed. "I'm lousy at writing.

But I use the telephone real well."

"Fine. I'll write. You call. Just keep in touch."

"You bet I will."

He jumped onto the truck as Randy was backing it out and stood on the running board and waved to her one more time before slipping inside the cab and closing the door. Jane watched him go and felt sorry that he was leaving. She wiped a tear from her cheek.

Suddenly, Toby was beside her with an arm thrown across Jane's shoulder. "You okay?"

"Yeah, I'm fine."

"Good, then we'd better help Andy get those decorations down before she starts looking for new roommates."

Within two hours, they had the whole student center cleared out. That is, all except the haunted house in the corner. They planned to save that mess for Gigi and Yolanda.

Meredith Pembroke came in just as they were leaving. She stood in the doorway with her hands on her hips, looking around her. "This looks great! You girls must have gotten an early start."

She came into the room and put her arms around Jane and Andy. "I wanted to tell you how nice everything looked. You did a super job with the decorations. I know the party wouldn't have been a success without your help."

"Well, actually, Andy is the one who deserves the credit for that," Jane said.

"And I wasn't talking about the haunted house fiasco," Meredith said, smiling.

"Neither was I," Jane confessed. "Actually, Andy did most of the work this week, and I just didn't want to let that slip by without telling you."

"Well, regardless of who did what, it looked terrific. I'm very pleased, girls. Why don't you stop by my room later this afternoon for a little tea party? I'll even bake some chocolate chip cookies."

"We wouldn't miss it," Toby said. Her mouth was already watering.

"Good. Well, I'd better see if I can find Dee and Maggie."

"They're in the kitchen," Andy said. "I don't know where Gigi and Yolanda are. We haven't seen them yet this morning."

"Okay. Thanks again, girls." Meredith disappeared into the kitchen.

"She sure turned out to be neat for as crummy as she started out, huh?" Andy asked. Each girl thought back to those early days when Meredith was new to Canby Hall and had about as much compassion as Attila the Hun. But a series of events, culminating in Toby's fall from a horse, brought her back down to earth. Now the girls wouldn't have traded her for anything.

As they came out of the student center, Toby saw Neal's car pull up and felt her pulse quicken. "See you guys later," she said as she cut across the grass to meet him. He put one arm around her and waved a friendly hello to Jane and Andy with the other.

"I wanted to stop by before I left," he said.

"I'm glad you did." He slid his arm down her shoulders and took hold of her hand. They walked across the grass, which was dry and brown beneath their feet. The fallen leaves had all scattered and blown away. Things looked so desolate now. It would be a long time until spring, Toby thought as she looked at the stark limbs above her. She shivered.

Neal stopped and pulled her to him. "Are you cold?"

"A little, I guess."

"You want to go back to Baker?"

"No."

"Good." He held her tightly, and she closed her eyes so she could remember this moment after he was gone. "I've been thinking," he said.

"Yeah?"

"I don't think we should wait so long to see each other next time."

"Me, neither," Toby said, looking into his eyes. He moved his face closer to hers. His lips briefly brushed her own, and she wrapped her arms more tightly around him and held him to her. Why couldn't he go to Oakley Prep like Cary did? Boston seemed so far away.

"I really should be going," he said reluctantly. He took her by the hand and they walked back to his car. "I'll try to come down next month. I'll call you. Okay?"

Toby nodded and said, "Okay." He opened his car door, but instead of getting in, he leaned against the car and pulled her to him again.

"I wish I didn't have to go." He took her face in his hands and gave her a tender good-bye kiss. He got into his car and rolled the window down so Toby could lean in and say good-bye.

"I think I need one more if it has to last me for a month," she said, and then she kissed him. The look of surprise on Neal's face made her laugh. Then Neal began to laugh, too.

"Why, October Houston, I do believe you're warming up a little." She stood up and let him pull away from the curb. He waved at her before he closed his window. She stood, arms folded against the November wind, and watched until his car was no longer visible.

* * *

Andy flopped down on her bed and sighed with relief. "You know, this has been some crazy weekend."

"It's been some crazy week," Jane said. "I'm really sorry I didn't do my part with the Halloween party. It's just that when we signed up to do it, I had no idea that so many other things were going to happen this week."

"Well, we all pulled together and got it done in the end," Andy said, sitting up on the bed, "and that's what counts."

"I wonder if Gigi's been over to clean up her mess, yet?" Toby asked. A smile crept across her face. "That was really something to see when the whole thing came down like a collapsible toy. People were running everywhere, and the funniest of all was Gigi crawling out of there looking like she'd been hit by a tornado."

"I'm just glad no one got hurt," Andy said with a shudder. "It would have been my fault. I'm the one who started it all."

"Wrong. Gigi started it all. Her and her dumb rats. I wish you could have seen the look on P.A.'s face when that little guy ran over the top of her shoe trying to get out of the student center. For a minute there, I thought we were going to have to perform a little CPR on old P.A.," Toby laughed.

In spite of herself, Andy laughed, too. "I

just hope Gigi's revenge isn't as bad as it sounds."

"Well, there's one thing for sure," Jane said. "Gigi got one clear victory out of this whole thing. She got Cary."

"Oh, come on, Jane," Andy said. "You don't really believe that he'd be interested in a girl like that, do you?"

"I saw him last night, just before everything fell apart. He and Gigi had been in the haunted house. He still had her lipstick on his lips."

"She probably attacked him," Toby said. "I know I'd sure hate to be alone in the dark with her."

Andy looked at Toby critically. "I think you're probably safe."

"Yeah," Jane sighed. "But poor Cary isn't."

Dee knocked on the door and stuck her head in. "Hey, you guys. You ready to go up to Merry's?"

"Sure," Toby said jumping from her bed. "You don't have to ask me twice."

"No kidding," Jane teased.

The smell of the freshly baked cookies seeped out from under the door and tantalized their senses while they waited for Meredith to answer the door.

"Come on in," she called. The girls opened the door just as she was taking the last tray of cookies from the oven. "Get them while they're hot," she said.

All five girls rushed over and gingerly lifted the soft, warm cookies from the plate. "Milk? Tea? Coke? What'll it be?" Meredith asked.

The girls all sat crowded around Meredith's small kitchen table where they could easily reach the cookies. The plate was nearly empty. "We're not saving you any for later," Andy said.

"That's okay. I don't need any for later. You guys go ahead and eat these up, or I'll do it myself and hate you for it. I've already put a plate aside for Gigi and Yolanda."

"Yeah, where are they anyway?" Dee asked, though she really didn't care.

"They got a late start cleaning up, and she said they'd try to stop by later."

"That was lucky timing on our part," Jane said.

Meredith let that comment slip by. After working with Gigi these last two weeks, she could see why the girls weren't too crazy about her.

After Toby had eaten the last cookie, the girls took that as their cue to leave. "Thanks for letting us make pigs of ourselves," Toby said.

"Well, not all of us made pigs of ourselves," Jane reminded Toby.

"That's okay," Meredith laughed. "I wanted you to enjoy the cookies. I really appreciate all the hard work you put into the party. You girls are terrific!" She hugged each girl on her way out. "Thanks again," she called as she closed the door behind them.

"Well, I can skip dinner tonight," Toby said.

"I'd think you could skip several meals with all the cookies you put away in there." Jane patted Toby's stomach.

They came around the corner of the fourth floor and a girl named Karen was just coming from their room. "Hey, Jane, I'm glad I found you. A certain guy has been in the lobby for the last half hour waiting for you. This is my third trip up here."

"Thanks," Jane said. What guy could that be? Beau would be on his way back to Texas by now. And Cary was probably helping Gigi clean up the mess from the dilapidated haunted house. She turned to Andy, "Do I look okay?"

"You look fine."

"Then I'll see you guys later." Jane ran off toward the stairs. She saw Cary sitting in the lobby near the window staring out at the barren campus. He looked so lonely. Her heart went out to him. She realized how difficult this past week must have been for him.

"Hi, Cary."

He stood up at the sound of her voice. "Jane. I've been waiting for you."

"I heard."

"I . . . uh. . . . Could we take a walk?"

"Sure." Jane didn't have her coat, but she was afraid if she ran back up the room to get it that Gigi might come in on her way up to Meredith's. She wasn't taking a chance of making things easier for Gigi.

The late afternoon sun did little to cut the bite of the November air. Jane crossed her arms in front of her as they walked. She longed for Cary's arm around her instead.

"I just wanted to explain about last night. It wasn't what you think with Gigi. . . ."

"I know. And you had every right to be with someone else if you wanted."

"But that's just it. I didn't want to be with anyone else."

Jane stopped and looked into his deep blue eyes. "You didn't?"

"No." He put his arms around her and pulled her into the welcome warmth of his body. "And I realized I didn't want you with anyone else, either."

"I won't be," Jane said. His mouth found hers and they kissed. Jane was aware of the difference in the way he and Beau felt in her arms. Beau was stronger, but Cary was gentler. Yet each one was special to her. She remembered her farewell with Beau just a few hours ago. She had to tell Cary everything this time. She wasn't going to get herself into another mess like she'd had all week.

"Cary, I want you to know that I'm still going to write to Beau."

"What does that mean, exactly?" Cary said stepping back from her and looking at her critically.

"Just that. He's going back to Texas to go on with his life, and I'm going to go on with mine. And you are a very important part of my life."

"I like that part. But I'm not so sure I like this writing him stuff."

"Well, look at it this way," Jane said as she linked her arm through his. "Texas is two thousand miles from here, and you're just down the road."

"Now *that* part, I like," Cary said. He placed his hand over Jane's. She looked into his glowing face and wasn't even aware of the cold anymore.

Toby and Andy were lying across their beds when Jane came back into the room. Toby looked over at Andy. "I'd say that must have been Cary downstairs."

"How did you know?" Jane asked.

"Because of the way you're smiling," Andy said. "I take it everything is all right."

"All right?" Jane sighed. "No, it's perfect."

She sat across her bed and pulled her knees into her chest.

"Does this mean Beau is out of the picture?" Andy asked, rolling over and sitting up where she could see Jane better.

"No. They both know I'm going to keep in touch with the other. It's just that now, I don't have to hide anything anymore."

"Honestly, Barrett," Toby said, getting off her bed and coming over to sit on the chair near Jane's bed. "You have got some kind of luck. You're the only person I know who could start out with two guys, look like you're going to lose both of them, and end up with two guys again."

"Guess I'm lucky," Jane smiled and rested her head on her knees. Her long blonde hair draped across her legs.

Andy got up and came over to sit on the edge of Jane's bed. "I'd say we're all pretty lucky. Just think about it. We could have gotten stuck with someone like Gigi for a roommate and instead we got each other."

"Yeah," Toby sighed. Then she broke into a wide smile. "We didn't think we were so lucky at first, though, did we?"

Jane began to laugh. "I remember the first time I saw you. I thought, Oh no, I'm going to be rooming with Calamity Jane."

"And I thought you two were the weirdest girls at Canby Hall," Andy said. Their laughter died out and was replaced by the silence of their reflections of their first meeting just over a year ago.

Andy looked at Jane and Toby. "Isn't it funny how you can get so close to someone in just a year? I feel like I've known you two all my life."

Jane reached out and touched Andy's shoulder. "Yeah, I know what you mean." She leaned forward on the bed and put her arms over Andy's and Toby's shoulders. "We may not have known each other that long, but we'll always be friends — for the rest of our lives!"

There's going to be a royal wedding, and the girls of Room 407 are invited! Read The Girls of Canby Hall #31, HERE COMES THE BRIDESMAID.